ROALD DAHL

The Witches, Esio Trot, The Twits
The Giraffe and the Pelly and Me

ROALD DAHL

The Witches, Esio Trot, The Twits
The Giraffe and the Pelly and Me

Illustrated by Quentin Blake

LEOPARD

This edition published in 1999 by
Leopard, a division of Random House UK Ltd
20 Vauxhall Road, London, SW1V 2SA

All four titles first published by
Jonathan Cape

The Witches
Text © 1983 Felicity Dahl and the other Executives
of the Estate of Roald Dahl.
Illustrations © 1983 Quentin Blake

Esio Trot
Text © 1990 Felicity Dahl and the other Executives
of the Estate of Roald Dahl.
Illustrations © 1990 Quentin Blake

The Twits
Text © 1980 Felicity Dahl and the other Executives
of the Estate of Roald Dahl.
Illustrations © 1980 Quentin Blake

The Giraffe and the Pelly and Me
Text © 1985 Felicity Dahl and the other Executives
of the Estate of Roald Dahl.
This edition with new illustrations first published in 1992
Illustrations © 1992 Quentin Blake

ISBN 0 091 86878 5

Printed and bound in Great Britain by
Mackays of Chatham PLC, Chatham, Kent

Contents

Roald Dahl
The Witches

Illustrations by Quentin Blake

For Liccy

Contents

A Note about Witches

In fairy-tales, witches always wear silly black hats and black cloaks, and they ride on broomsticks.

But this is not a fairy-tale. This is about REAL WITCHES.

The most important thing you should know about REAL WITCHES is this. Listen very carefully. Never forget what is coming next.

REAL WITCHES dress in ordinary clothes and look very much like ordinary women. They live in ordinary houses and they work in ORDINARY JOBS.

That is why they are so hard to catch.

A REAL WITCH hates children with a red-hot sizzling hatred that is more sizzling and red-hot than any hatred you could possibly imagine.

A REAL WITCH spends all her time plotting to get rid of the children in her particular territory. Her passion is to do away with them, one by one. It is all she thinks about the whole day long. Even if she is working as a cashier in a supermarket or typing letters for a businessman or driving round in a fancy car (and she could be doing any of these things), her mind will always be plotting and scheming and churning and burning and whizzing and phizzing with murderous bloodthirsty thoughts.

"Which child," she says to herself all day long, "exactly which child shall I choose for my next squelching?"

A REAL WITCH gets the same pleasure from squelching a child as *you* get from eating a plateful of strawberries and thick cream.

She reckons on doing away with one child a week. Anything less than that and she becomes grumpy.

One child a week is fifty-two a year.

Squish them and squiggle them and make them disappear.

That is the motto of all witches.

Very carefully a victim is chosen. Then the witch stalks the wretched child like a hunter stalking a little bird in the forest. She treads softly.

She moves quietly. She gets closer and closer. Then at last, when everything is ready . . . *phwisst!* . . . and she swoops! Sparks fly. Flames leap. Oil boils. Rats howl. Skin shrivels. And the child disappears.

A witch, you must understand, does not knock children on the head or stick knives into them or shoot at them with a pistol. People who do those things get caught by the police.

A witch never gets caught. Don't forget that she has magic in her fingers and devilry dancing in her blood. She can make stones jump about like frogs and she can make tongues of flame go flickering across the surface of the water.

These magic powers are very frightening.

Luckily, there are not a great number of REAL WITCHES in the world today. But there are still quite enough to make you nervous. In England, there are probably about one hundred of them altogether. Some countries have more, others have not quite so many. No country in the world is completely free from WITCHES.

A witch is always a woman.

I do not wish to speak badly about women. Most women are lovely. But the fact remains that all witches *are* women. There is no such thing as a male witch.

On the other hand, a ghoul is always a male. So indeed is a barghest. Both are dangerous. But neither of them is half as dangerous as a REAL WITCH.

As far as children are concerned, a REAL WITCH is

easily the most dangerous of all the living creatures on earth. What makes her doubly dangerous is the fact that she doesn't *look* dangerous. Even when you know all the secrets (you will hear about those in a minute), you can still never be quite sure whether it is a witch you are gazing at or just a kind lady. If a tiger were able to make himself look like a large dog with a waggy tail, you would probably go up and pat him on the head. And that would be the end of you. It is the same with witches. They all look like nice ladies.

Kindly examine the picture opposite. Which lady is the witch? That is a difficult question, but it is one that every child must try to answer.

For all you know, a witch might be living next door to you right now.

Or she might be the woman with the bright eyes who sat opposite you on the bus this morning.

She might be the lady with the dazzling smile who offered you a sweet from a white paper bag in the street before lunch.

She might even – and this will make you jump – she might even be your lovely school-teacher who is reading these words to you at this very moment. Look carefully at that teacher. Perhaps she is smiling at the absurdity of such a suggestion. Don't let that put you off. It could be part of her cleverness.

I am not, of course, telling you for one second that your teacher actually is a witch. All I am saying is that she *might* be one. It is most unlikely. But — and here comes the big "but" — *it is not impossible.*

Oh, if only there were a way of telling for sure whether a woman was a witch or not, then we could round them all up and put them in the meat-grinder. Unhappily, there is no such way. But there *are* a number of little signals you can look out for, little quirky habits that all witches have in common, and if you know about these, if you remember them always, then you might just possibly manage to escape from being squelched before you are very much older.

My Grandmother

I myself had two separate encounters with witches before I was eight years old. From the first I escaped unharmed, but on the second occasion I was not so lucky. Things happened to me that will probably make you scream when you read about them. That can't be helped. The truth must be told. The fact that I am still here and able to speak to you (however peculiar I may look) is due entirely to my wonderful grandmother.

My grandmother was Norwegian. The Norwegians know all about witches, for Norway, with its black forests and icy mountains, is where the first witches came from. My father and my mother were also Norwegian, but because my father had a business in England, I had been born there and had lived there and had started going to an English school. Twice a year, at Christmas and in the summer, we went back to Norway to visit my grandmother. This old lady, as far as I could gather, was just about the only surviving relative we had on either side of our family. She was my mother's mother and I absolutely adored her. When she and I were together we spoke in either Norwegian or in English. It didn't matter which. We were equally fluent in both languages, and I have to admit that I felt closer to her than to my mother.

Soon after my seventh birthday, my parents took me as usual to spend Christmas with my grandmother in Norway. And it was over there, while my father and mother and I were driving in icy weather just north of Oslo, that our car skidded off the road and went tumbling down into a rocky ravine. My parents were killed. I was firmly strapped into the back seat and received only a cut on the forehead.

I won't go into the horrors of that terrible afternoon. I still get the shivers when I think about it. I finished up, of course, back in my grandmother's house with her arms around me tight and both of us crying the whole night long.

"What are we going to do now?" I asked her through the tears.

"You will stay here with me," she said, "and I will look after you."

"Aren't I going back to England?"

"No," she said. "I could never do that. Heaven shall take my soul, but Norway shall keep my bones."

The very next day, in order that we might both try to forget our great sadness, my grandmother started telling me stories. She was a wonderful story-teller and I was enthralled by everything she told me. But I didn't become really excited until she got on to the subject of witches. She was apparently a great expert on these creatures and she made it very clear to me that her witch stories, unlike most of the others, were not imaginary tales. They were all true. They were the *gospel* truth. They were history. Everything she was telling me about witches had actually happened and I had better believe it. What was worse, what was far, far worse, was that witches were still with us. They were all around us and I had better believe that, too.

"Are you *really* being truthful, Grandmamma? *Really* and *truly* truthful?"

"My darling," she said, "you won't last long in this world if you don't know how to spot a witch when you see one."

"But you told me that witches look like ordinary women, Grandmamma. So how can I spot them?"

"You must listen to me," my grandmother said. "You must remember everything I tell you. After that, all you can do is cross your heart and pray to heaven and hope for the best."

We were in the big living-room of her house in Oslo and I was ready for bed. The curtains were never drawn in that house, and through the windows I could see huge snowflakes falling slowly on to an outside world that was as black as tar. My grandmother was tremendously old and wrinkled, with a massive wide body which was smothered in grey lace. She sat there majestic in her armchair, filling every inch of it. Not even a mouse could have squeezed in to sit beside her. I myself, just seven years old, was crouched on the floor at her feet, wearing pyjamas, dressing-gown and slippers.

"You swear you aren't pulling my leg?" I kept saying to her. "You swear you aren't just pretending?"

"Listen," she said, "I have known no less than five children who have simply vanished off the face of this earth, never to be seen again. The witches took them."

"I still think you're just trying to frighten me," I said.

"I am trying to make sure you don't go the same way," she said. "I love you and I want you to stay with me."

"Tell me about the children who disappeared," I said.

My grandmother was the only grandmother I ever met who smoked cigars. She lit one now, a

19

long black cigar that smelt of burning rubber. "The first child I knew who disappeared", she said, "was called Ranghild Hansen. Ranghild was about eight at the time, and she was playing with her little sister on the lawn. Their mother, who was baking bread in the kitchen, came outside for a breath of air. 'Where's Ranghild?' she asked.

" 'She went away with the tall lady,' the little sister said.

" 'What tall lady?' the mother said.

" 'The tall lady in white gloves,' the little sister said. 'She took Ranghild by the hand and led her away.' No one", my grandmother said, "ever saw Ranghild again."

"Didn't they search for her?" I asked.

"They searched for miles around. Everyone in the town helped, but they never found her."

"What happened to the other four children?" I asked.

"They vanished just as Ranghild did."

"How, Grandmamma? How did they vanish?"

"In every case a strange lady was seen outside the house, just before it happened."

"But how did they vanish?" I asked.

"The second one was very peculiar," my grand-mother said. "There was a family called Christian-sen. They lived up on Holmenkollen, and they had an old oil-painting in the living-room which they were very proud of. The painting showed some ducks in the yard outside a farmhouse. There were no people in the painting, just a flock of ducks on a grassy farmyard and the farmhouse in the back-

ground. It was a large painting and rather pretty. Well, one day their daughter Solveg came home from school eating an apple. She said a nice lady had given it to her on the street. The next morning little Solveg was not in her bed. The parents searched everywhere but they couldn't find her. Then all of a sudden her father shouted, 'There she is! That's Solveg feeding the ducks!' He was pointing at the oil-painting, and sure enough Solveg was in it. She was standing in the farmyard in the act of throwing bread to the ducks out of a basket. The father rushed up to the painting and touched her. But that didn't help. She was simply a part of the painting, just a picture painted on the canvas."

"Did *you* ever see that painting, Grandmamma, with the little girl in it?"

"Many times," my grandmother said. "And the peculiar thing was that little Solveg kept changing her position in the picture. One day she would actually be inside the farmhouse and you could see her face looking out of the window. Another day she would be far over to the left with a duck in her arms."

"Did you see her moving in the picture, Grandmamma?"

"Nobody did. Wherever she was, whether outside feeding the ducks or inside looking out of the window, she was always motionless, just a figure painted in oils. It was all very odd," my grandmother said. "Very odd indeed. And what was most odd of all was that as the years went by, she kept growing older in the picture. In ten years, the small girl had become a young woman. In thirty years, she was middle-aged. Then all at once, fifty-four years after it all happened, she disappeared from the picture altogether."

"You mean she died?" I said.

"Who knows?" my grandmother said. "Some very mysterious things go on in the world of witches."

"That's two you've told me about," I said. "What happened to the third one?"

"The third one was little Birgit Svenson," my grandmother said. "She lived just across the road from us. One day she started growing feathers all over her body. Within a month, she had turned

23

into a large white chicken. Her parents kept her for years in a pen in the garden. She even laid eggs."

"What colour eggs?" I said.

"Brown ones," my grandmother said. "Biggest eggs I've ever seen in my life. Her mother made omelettes out of them. Delicious they were."

I gazed up at my grandmother who sat there like some ancient queen on her throne. Her eyes were misty-grey and they seemed to be looking at something many miles away. The cigar was the only real thing about her at that moment, and the smoke it made billowed round her head in blue clouds.

"But the little girl who became a chicken didn't disappear?" I said.

"No, not Birgit. She lived on for many years laying her brown eggs."

"You said all of them disappeared."

"I made a mistake," my grandmother said. "I am getting old. I can't remember everything."

"What happened to the fourth child?" I asked.

"The fourth was a boy called Harald," my grandmother said. "One morning his skin went all greyish-yellow. Then it became hard and crackly, like the shell of a nut. By evening, the boy had turned to stone."

"Stone?" I said. "You mean real stone?"

"Granite," she said. "I'll take you to see him if you like. They still keep him in the house. He stands in the hall, a little stone statue. Visitors lean their umbrellas up against him."

Although I was very young, I was not prepared to believe everything my grandmother told me. And yet she spoke with such conviction, with such utter seriousness, and with never a smile on her face or a twinkle in her eye, that I found myself beginning to wonder.

"Go on, Grandmamma," I said.

"You told me there were five altogether. What happened to the last one?"

"Would you like a puff of my cigar?" she said.

"I'm only seven, Grandmamma."

"I don't care what age you are," she said. "You'll never catch a cold if you smoke cigars."

"What about number five, Grandmamma?"

"Number five", she said, chewing the end of her

25

cigar as though it were a delicious asparagus, "was rather an interesting case. A nine-year-old boy called Leif was summer-holidaying with his family on the fjord, and the whole family was picnicking and swimming off some rocks on one of those little islands. Young Leif dived into the water and his father, who was watching him, noticed that he stayed under for an unusually long time. When he came to the surface at last, he wasn't Leif any more."

"What was he, Grandmamma?"

"He was a porpoise."

"He wasn't! He couldn't have been!"

"He was a lovely young porpoise," she said. "And as friendly as could be."

"Grandmamma," I said.

"Yes, my darling?"

"Did he really and truly turn into a porpoise?"

"Absolutely," she said. "I knew his mother well. She told me all about it. She told me how Leif the Porpoise stayed with them all that afternoon giving his brothers and sisters rides on his back. They had a wonderful time. Then he waved a flipper at them and swam away, never to be seen again."

"But Grandmamma," I said, "how did they know that the porpoise was actually Leif?"

"He talked to them," my grandmother said. "He laughed and joked with them all the time he was giving them rides."

"But wasn't there a most tremendous fuss when this happened?" I asked.

"Not much," my grandmother said. "You must remember that here in Norway we are used to that sort of thing. There are witches everywhere. There's probably one living in our street this very moment. It's time you went to bed."

"A witch wouldn't come in through my window in the night, would she?" I asked, quaking a little.

"No," my grandmother said. "A witch will never do silly things like climbing up drainpipes or breaking into people's houses. You'll be quite safe in your bed. Come along. I'll tuck you in."

How to Recognise a Witch

The next evening, after my grandmother had given me my bath, she took me once again into the living-room for another story.

"Tonight," the old woman said, "I am going to tell you how to recognise a witch when you see one."

"Can you always be sure?" I asked.

"No," she said, "you can't. And that's the trouble. But you can make a pretty good guess."

She was dropping cigar ash all over her lap, and I hoped she wasn't going to catch on fire before she'd told me how to recognise a witch.

"In the first place," she said, "a REAL WITCH is certain always to be wearing gloves when you meet her."

"Surely not *always*," I said. "What about in the summer when it's hot?"

"Even in the summer," my grandmother said. "She has to. Do you want to know why?"

"Why?" I said.

"Because she doesn't have finger-nails. Instead of finger-nails, she has thin curvy claws, like a cat, and she wears the gloves to hide them. Mind you, lots of very respectable women wear gloves, especially in winter, so this doesn't help you very much."

28

"Mamma used to wear gloves," I said.

"Not in the house," my grandmother said. "Witches wear gloves even in the house. They only take them off when they go to bed."

"How do you know all this, Grandmamma?"

"Don't interrupt," she said. "Just take it all in. The second thing to remember is that a REAL WITCH is always bald."

"*Bald?*" I said.

"Bald as a boiled egg," my grandmother said.

I was shocked. There was something indecent about a bald woman. "Why are they bald, Grandmamma?"

"Don't ask me why," she snapped. "But you can take it from me that not a single hair grows on a witch's head."

"How horrid!"

"Disgusting," my grandmother said.

"If she's bald, she'll be easy to spot," I said.

"Not at all," my grandmother said. "A REAL WITCH always wears a wig to hide her baldness. She wears a first-class wig. And it is almost impossible to tell a really first-class wig from ordinary hair unless you give it a pull to see if it comes off."

"Then that's what I'll have to do," I said.

"Don't be foolish," my grandmother said. "You can't go round pulling at the hair of every lady you meet, even if she *is* wearing gloves. Just you try it and see what happens."

"So that doesn't help much either," I said.

"None of these things is any good on its own," my grandmother said. "It's only when you put them all together that they begin to make a little sense. Mind you," my grandmother went on, "these wigs do cause a rather serious problem for witches."

"What problem, Grandmamma?"

"They make the scalp itch most terribly," she said. "You see, when an actress wears a wig, or if you or I were to wear a wig, we would be putting it on over our own hair, but a witch has to put it straight on to her naked scalp. And the underneath of a wig is always very rough and scratchy. It sets up a frightful itch on the bald skin. It causes nasty sores on the head. Wig-rash, the witches call it. And it doesn't half itch."

"What other things must I look for to recognise a witch?" I asked.

"Look for the nose-holes," my grandmother said. "Witches have slightly larger nose-holes than ordinary people. The rim of each nose-hole is pink and curvy, like the rim of a certain kind of sea-shell."

"Why do they have such big nose-holes?" I asked.

"For smelling with," my grandmother said. "A REAL WITCH has the most amazing powers of smell. She can actually smell out a child who is standing on the other side of the street on a pitch-black night."

"She couldn't smell me," I said. "I've just had a bath."

"Oh yes she could," my grandmother said. "The cleaner you happen to be, the more smelly you are to a witch."

"That can't be true," I said.

"An absolutely clean child gives off the most ghastly stench to a witch," my grandmother said. "The dirtier you are, the less you smell."

"But that doesn't make sense, Grandmamma."

"Oh yes it does," my grandmother said. "It isn't the *dirt* that the witch is smelling. It is *you*. The smell that drives a witch mad actually comes right out of your own skin. It comes oozing out of your skin in waves, and these waves, stink-waves the witches call them, go floating through the air and hit the witch right smack in her nostrils. They send her reeling."

"Now wait a minute, Grandmamma . . . "

"Don't interrupt," she said. "The point is this. When you haven't washed for a week and your skin is all covered over with dirt, then quite obviously the stink-waves cannot come oozing out nearly so strongly."

"I shall never have a bath again," I said.

"Just don't have one too often," my grandmother said. "Once a month is quite enough for a sensible child."

It was at moments like these that I loved my grandmother more than ever.

"Grandmamma," I said, "if it's a dark night, how can a witch smell the difference between a child and a grown-up?"

"Because grown-ups don't give out stink-waves," she said. "Only children do that."

"But I don't *really* give out stink-waves, do I?" I

said. "I'm not giving them out at this very moment, am I?"

"Not to me you aren't," my grandmother said. "To me you are smelling like raspberries and cream. But to a witch you would be smelling absolutely disgusting."

"What would I be smelling of?" I asked.

"Dogs' droppings," my grandmother said.

I reeled. I was stunned. *"Dogs' droppings!"* I cried. "I am *not* smelling of dogs' droppings! I don't believe it! I *won't* believe it!"

"What's more," my grandmother said, speaking with a touch of relish, "to a witch you'd be smelling of *fresh* dogs' droppings."

"That simply is not true!" I cried. "I know I am not smelling of dogs' droppings, stale or fresh!"

"There's no point in arguing about it," my grandmother said. "It's a fact of life."

I was outraged. I simply couldn't bring myself to believe what my grandmother was telling me.

"So if you see a woman holding her nose as she passes you in the street," she went on, "that woman could easily be a witch."

I decided to change the subject. "Tell me what else to look for in a witch," I said.

"The eyes," my grandmother said. "Look carefully at the eyes, because the eyes of a REAL WITCH are different from yours and mine. Look in the middle of each eye where there is normally a little black dot. If she is a witch, the black dot will keep changing colour, and you will see fire and you will see ice dancing right in the very centre of the coloured dot. It will send shivers running all over your skin."

My grandmother leant back in her chair and sucked away contentedly at her foul black cigar. I squatted on the floor, staring up at her, fascinated. She was not smiling. She looked deadly serious.

"Are there other things?" I asked her.

"Of course there are other things," my grandmother said. "You don't seem to understand that witches are not actually women at all. They *look* like women. They talk like women. And they are able to act like women. But in actual fact, they are totally different animals. They are demons in human shape. That is why they have claws and bald heads and queer noses and peculiar eyes, all of which they have to conceal as best they can from the rest of the world."

"What else is different about them, Grand-mamma?"

"The feet," she said. "Witches never have toes."

"No toes!" I cried. "Then what do they have?"

"They just have feet," my grandmother said. "The feet have square ends with no toes on them at all."

"Does that make it difficult to walk?" I asked.

"Not at all," my grandmother said. "But it does give them a problem with their shoes. All ladies like to wear small rather pointed shoes, but a witch, whose feet are very wide and square at the ends, has the most awful job squeezing her feet into those neat little pointed shoes."

"Why doesn't she wear wide comfy shoes with square ends?" I asked.

"She dare not," my grandmother said. "Just as she hides her baldness with a wig, she must also hide her ugly witch's feet by squeezing them into pretty shoes."

"Isn't that terribly uncomfortable?" I said.

34

"Extremely uncomfortable," my grandmother said. "But she has to put up with it."

"If she's wearing ordinary shoes, it won't help me to recognise her, will it, Grandmamma?"

"I'm afraid it won't," my grandmother said. "You might possibly see her limping very slightly, but only if you were watching closely."

"Are those the only differences then, Grand-mamma?"

"There's one more," my grandmother said. "Just one more."

"What is it, Grandmamma?"

"Their spit is blue."

"Blue!" I cried. "Not blue! Their spit can't be *blue!*"

"Blue as a bilberry," she said.

"You don't mean it, Grandmamma! Nobody can have blue spit!"

"Witches can," she said.

"Is it like ink?" I asked.

"Exactly," she said. "They even use it to write with. They use those old-fashioned pens that have nibs and they simply lick the nib."

"Can you *notice* the blue spit, Grandmamma? If a witch was talking to me, would I be able to notice it?"

"Only if you looked carefully," my grandmother said. "If you looked very carefully you would

35

probably see a slight blueish tinge on her teeth. But it doesn't show much."

"It would if she spat," I said.

"Witches never spit," my grandmother said. "They daren't."

I couldn't believe my grandmother would be lying to me. She went to church every morning of the week and she said grace before every meal, and somebody who did that would never tell lies. I was beginning to believe every word she spoke.

"So there you are," my grandmother said. "That's about all I can tell you. None of it is very helpful. You can still never be absolutely sure whether a woman is a witch or not just by looking at her. But if she is wearing the gloves, if she has the large nose-holes, the queer eyes and the hair that looks as though it might be a wig, and if she has a blueish tinge on her teeth – if she has all of these things, then you run like mad."

"Grandmamma," I said, "when you were a little girl, did *you* ever meet a witch?"

"Once," my grandmother said. "Only once."

"What happened?"

"I'm not going to tell you," she said. "It would frighten you out of your skin and give you bad dreams."

"Please tell me," I begged.

"No," she said. "Certain things are too horrible to talk about."

"Does it have something to do with your missing thumb?" I asked.

Suddenly, her old wrinkled lips shut tight as a

36

pair of tongs and the hand that held the cigar (which had no thumb on it) began to quiver very slightly.

I waited. She didn't look at me. She didn't speak. All of a sudden she had shut herself off completely. The conversation was finished.

"Goodnight, Grandmamma," I said, rising from the floor and kissing her on the cheek.

She didn't move. I crept out of the room and went to my bedroom.

The Grand High Witch

The next day, a man in a black suit arrived at the house carrying a brief-case, and he held a long conversation with my grandmother in the living-room. I was not allowed in while he was there, but when at last he went away, my grandmother came in to me, walking very slowly and looking very sad.

"That man was reading me your father's will," she said.

"What is a will?" I asked her.

"It is something you write before you die," she said. "And in it you say who is going to have your money and your property. But most important of all, it says who is going to look after your child if both the mother and father are dead."

A fearful panic took hold of me. "It did say you, Grandmamma?" I cried. "I don't have to go to somebody else, do I?"

"No," she said. "Your father would never have done that. He has asked me to take care of you for as long as I live, but he has also asked that I take you back to your own house in England. He wants us to stay there."

"But why?" I said. "Why can't we stay here in Norway? You would hate to live anywhere else! You told me you would!"

"I know," she said. "But there are a lot of complications with money and with the house that you wouldn't understand. Also, it said in the will that although all your family is Norwegian, you were born in England and you have started your education there and he wants you to continue going to English schools."

"Oh Grandmamma!" I cried. "*You* don't want to go and live in our English house, I know you don't!"

"Of course I don't," she said. "But I am afraid I must. The will said that your mother felt the same way about it, and it is important to respect the wishes of the parents."

There was no way out of it. We had to go to England, and my grandmother started making arrangements at once. "Your next school term begins in a few days," she said, "so we don't have any time to waste."

On the evening before we left for England, my grandmother got on to her favourite subject once again. "There are not as many witches in England as there are in Norway," she said.

"I'm sure I won't meet one," I said.

"I sincerely hope you won't," she said, "because those English witches are probably the most vicious in the whole world."

As she sat there smoking her foul cigar and talking away, I kept looking at the hand with the missing thumb. I couldn't help it. I was fascinated by it and I kept wondering what awful thing had happened that time when she had met a witch. It must have been something absolutely appalling and gruesome otherwise she would have told me about it. Maybe the thumb had been twisted off. Or perhaps she had been forced to jam her thumb down the spout of a boiling kettle until it was steamed away. Or did someone pull it out of her hand like a tooth? I couldn't help trying to guess.

"Tell me what those English witches do, Grandmamma," I said.

"Well," she said, sucking away at her stinking cigar, "their favourite ruse is to mix up a powder that will turn a child into some creature or other that all grown-ups hate."

"What sort of a creature, Grandmamma?"

"Often it's a slug," she said. "A slug is one of their favourites. Then the grown-ups step on the slug and squish it without knowing it's a child."

"That's perfectly beastly!" I cried.

"Or it might be a flea," my grandmother said. "They might turn you into a flea, and without realising what she was doing your own mother would get out the flea-powder and then it's goodbye you."

"You're making me nervous, Grandmamma. I don't think I want to go back to England."

"I've known English witches", she went on, "who have turned children into pheasants and then sneaked the pheasants up into the woods the very day before the pheasant-shooting season opened."

"Owch," I said. "So they get shot?"

"Of course they get shot," she said. "And then they get plucked and roasted and eaten for supper."

I pictured myself as a pheasant flying frantically over the men with the guns, swerving and dipping as the guns exploded below me.

"Yes," my grandmother said, "it gives the English witches great pleasure to stand back and watch the grown-ups doing away with their own children."

"I really don't want to go to England, Grandmamma."

"Of course you don't," she said. "Nor do I. But I'm afraid we've got to."

"Are witches different in every country?" I asked.

"Completely different," my grandmother said. "But I don't know much about the other countries."

"Don't you even know about America?" I asked.

"Not really," she answered. "Although I have heard it said that over there the witches are able to make the grown-ups eat their own children."

"Never!" I cried. "Oh no, Grandmamma! That couldn't be true!"

"I don't know whether it's true or not," she said. "It's only a rumour I've heard."

"But how could they possibly make them eat their own children?" I asked.

"By turning them into hot-dogs," she said. "That wouldn't be too difficult for a clever witch."

"Does every single country in the world have its witches?" I asked.

"Wherever you find people, you find witches," my grandmother said. "There is a Secret Society of Witches in every country."

"And do they all know one another, Grandmamma?"

"They do not," she said. "A witch only knows the witches in her own country. She is strictly forbidden to communicate with any foreign witches. But an English witch, for example, will know all the other witches in England. They are all friends. They ring each other up. They swop deadly recipes. Goodness knows what else they talk about. I hate to think."

I sat on the floor, watching my grandmother. She put her cigar stub in the ashtray and folded her hands across her stomach. "Once a year," she went on, "the witches of each separate country hold their own secret meeting. They all get together in one place to receive a lecture from The Grand High Witch Of All The World."

"From *who*?" I cried.

"She is the ruler of them all," my grandmother said. "She is all-powerful. She is without mercy. All other witches are petrified of her. They see her only once a year at their Annual Meeting. She goes there to whip up excitement and enthusiasm, and to give orders. The Grand High Witch travels from country to country attending these Annual Meetings."

"Where do they have these meetings, Grandmamma?"

"There are all sorts of rumours," my grandmother answered. "I have heard it said that they just book into an hotel like any other group of women who are holding a meeting. I have also heard it said that some very peculiar things go on in the hotels they stay in. It is rumoured that the beds are never slept in, that there are burn marks on the bedroom carpets, that toads are discovered in the bathtubs, and that down in the kitchen the cook once found a baby crocodile swimming in his saucepan of soup."

My grandmother picked up her cigar and took another puff, inhaling the foul smoke deeply into her lungs.

"Where does The Grand High Witch live when she's at home?" I asked.

"Nobody knows," my grandmother said. "If we knew that, then she could be rooted out and destroyed. Witchophiles all over the world have spent their lives trying to discover the secret Headquarters of The Grand High Witch."

"What is a witchophile, Grandmamma?"

"A person who studies witches and knows a lot about them," my grandmother said.

"Are you a witchophile, Grandmamma?"

"I am a retired witchophile," she said. "I am too old to be active any longer. But when I was younger, I travelled all over the globe trying to track down The Grand High Witch. I never came even close to succeeding."

"Is she rich?" I asked.

"She's rolling," my grandmother said. "Simply rolling in money. Rumour has it that there is a machine in her headquarters which is exactly like the machine the government uses to print the bank-notes you and I use. After all, bank-notes are

44

only bits of paper with special designs and pictures on them. Anyone can make them who has the right machine and the right paper. My guess is that The Grand High Witch makes all the money she wants and she dishes it out to witches everywhere."

"What about foreign money?" I asked.

"Those machines can make *Chinese* money if you want them to," my grandmother said. "It's only a question of pressing the right button."

"But Grandmamma," I said, "if nobody has ever seen The Grand High Witch, how can you be so sure she exists?"

My grandmother gave me a long and very severe look. "Nobody has ever seen the Devil," she said, "but we know he exists."

The next morning, we sailed for England and soon I was back in the old family house in Kent, but this time with only my grandmother to look after me. Then the Easter Term began and every weekday I went to school and everything seemed to have come back to normal again.

Now at the bottom of our garden there was an enormous conker tree, and high up in its branches Timmy (my best friend) and I had started to build a magnificent tree-house. We were able to work on it only at the weekends, but we were getting along fine. We had begun with the floor, which we built by laying wide planks between two quite far-apart branches and nailing them down. Within a month, we had finished the floor. Then we constructed a wooden railing around the floor and that left only

the roof to be built. The roof was the difficult bit.

One Saturday afternoon when Timmy was in bed with 'flu, I decided to make a start on the roof all by myself. It was lovely being high up there in that conker tree, all alone with the pale young leaves coming out everywhere around me. It was like being in a big green cave. And the height made it extra exciting. My grandmother had told me that if I fell I would break a leg, and every time I looked down, I got a tingle along my spine.

I worked away, nailing the first plank on the roof. Then suddenly, out of the corner of my eye, I caught sight of a woman standing immediately below me. She was looking up at me and smiling in the most peculiar way. When most people smile, their lips go out sideways. This woman's lips went upwards and downwards, showing all her front teeth and gums. The gums were like raw meat.

It is always a shock to discover that you are being watched when you think you are alone.

And what was this strange woman doing in our garden anyway?

I noticed that she was wearing a small black hat and she had black gloves on her hands and the gloves came nearly up to her elbows.

Gloves! She was wearing *gloves!*

I froze all over.

"I have a present for you," she said, still staring at me, still smiling, still showing her teeth and gums.

I didn't answer.

47

"Come down out of that tree, little boy," she said, "and I shall give you the most exciting present you've ever had." Her voice had a curious rasping quality. It made a sort of metallic sound, as though her throat was full of drawing-pins.

Without taking her eyes from my face, she very slowly put one of those gloved hands into her purse and drew out a small green snake. She held it up for me to see.

"It's tame," she said.

The snake began to coil itself around her fore-arm. It was brilliant green.

"If you come down here, I shall give him to you," she said.

Oh Grandmamma, I thought, come and help me!

Then I panicked. I dropped the hammer and shot up that enormous tree like a monkey. I didn't stop until I was as high as I could possibly go, and there I stayed, quivering with fear. I couldn't see the woman now. There were layers and layers of leaves between her and me.

I stayed up there for hours and I kept very still. It began to grow dark. At last, I heard my grand-mother calling my name.

"I'm up here," I shouted back.

"Come down at once!" she called out. "It's past your suppertime."

"Grandmamma!" I shouted. "Has that woman gone?"

"What woman?" my grandmother called back.

"The woman in the black gloves!"

There was silence from below. It was the silence of somebody who was too stunned to speak.

"Grandmamma!" I shouted again. *"Has she gone?"*

"Yes," my grandmother answered at last. "She's gone. I'm here, my darling. I'll look after you. You can come down now."

I climbed down. I was trembling. My grand-mother enfolded me in her arms. "I've seen a witch," I said.

"Come inside," she said. "You'll be all right with me."

She led me into the house and gave me a cup of hot cocoa with lots of sugar in it. "Tell me everything," she said.

I told her.

By the time I had finished, it was my grandmother who was trembling. Her face was ashy grey and I saw her glance down at that hand of hers that didn't have a thumb. "You know what this means," she said. "It means that there is one of them in our district. From now on I'm not letting you walk alone to school."

"Do you think she could be after me specially?" I asked.

"No," she said. "I doubt that. One child is as good as any other to those creatures."

It is hardly surprising that after that I became a very witch-conscious little boy. If I happened to be alone on the road and saw a woman approaching who was wearing gloves, I would quickly skip across to the other side. And as the weather remained pretty cold during the whole of that month, nearly *everybody* was wearing gloves. Curiously enough though, I never saw the woman with the green snake again.

That was my first witch. But it wasn't my last.

Summer Holidays

The Easter holidays came and went, and the Summer Term began at school. My grandmother and I had already planned to take our summer holiday in Norway and we talked about almost nothing else every evening. She had booked a cabin for each of us on the boat from Newcastle to Oslo at the earliest possible moment after my school broke up, and from Oslo she was going to take me to a place she knew down on the south coast near Arendal where she had spent her own summer holidays as a child nearly eighty years ago.

"All day long," she said, "my brother and I were out in the rowing-boat. The whole coast is dotted with tiny islands and there's nobody on them. We used to explore them and dive into the sea off the lovely smooth granite rocks, and sometimes on the way out we would drop the anchor and fish for cod and whiting, and if we caught anything we would build a fire on an island and fry the fish in a pan for our lunch. There is no finer fish in the world than absolutely fresh cod."

"What did you use for bait, Grandmamma, when you went fishing?"

"Mussels," she said. "Everyone uses mussels for bait in Norway. And if we didn't catch any fish, we would boil the mussels in a saucepan and eat those."

"Were they good?"

"Delicious," she said. "Cook them in sea-water and they are tender and salty."

"What else did you do, Grandmamma?"

"We used to row out and wave to the shrimp-boats on their way home, and they would stop and give us a handful of shrimps each. The shrimps were still warm from having been just cooked, and we would sit in the rowing-boat peeling them and gobbling them up. The head was the best part."

"The head?" I said.

"You squeeze the head between your teeth and suck out the inside. It's marvellous. You and I will do all those things this summer, my darling," she said.

"Grandmamma," I said, "I can't wait. I simply can't wait to go."

"Nor can I," she said.

When there were only three weeks of the Summer Term left, an awful thing happened. My grandmother got pneumonia. She became very ill, and a trained nurse moved into the house to look after her. The doctor explained to me that pneumonia is not normally a dangerous illness nowadays because of penicillin, but when a person is more than eighty years old, as my grandmother was, then it is very dangerous indeed. He said he didn't even dare to move her to hospital in her condition, so she stayed in her bedroom and I hung about outside the door while oxygen cylinders and all sorts of other frightening things were taken in to her.

"Can I go in and see her?" I asked.

"No, dear," the nurse said. "Not at the moment."

A fat and jolly lady called Mrs Spring, who used to come and clean our house every day, also moved in and slept in the house. Mrs Spring looked after me and cooked my meals. I liked her very much, but she wasn't a patch on my grandmother for telling stories.

One evening, about ten days later, the doctor came downstairs and said to me, "You can go in and see her now, but only for a short time. She's been asking for you."

I flew up the stairs and burst into my grandmother's room and threw myself into her arms.

"Hey there," the nurse said. "Be careful with her."

"Will you be all right now, Grandmamma?" I asked.

"The worst is over," she said. "I'll soon be up again."

"Will she?" I said to the nurse.

"Oh yes," the nurse answered, smiling. "She told us she simply had to get better because she had to look after you."

I gave her another hug.

"They won't let me have a cigar," she said. "But you wait till they're gone."

"She's a tough old bird," the nurse said. "We'll have her up in another week."

The nurse was right. Within a week, my grandmother was thumping around the house with her gold-topped cane and interfering with Mrs Spring's cooking. "I thank you for all your help, Mrs Spring," she said, "but you can go home now."

"Oh, no I can't," Mrs Spring said. "Doctor told me to see that you take it very easy for the next few days."

The doctor said more than that. He dropped a bombshell on my grandmother and me by telling us that on no account were we to risk the journey to Norway this summer.

"Rubbish!" my grandmother cried. "I've promised him we'll go!"

"It's too far," the doctor said. "It would be very dangerous. But I'll tell you what you *can* do. You can take your grandson to a nice hotel on the

54

south coast of England instead. The sea air is just what you need."

"Oh no!" I said.

"Do you want your grandmother to die?" the doctor asked me.

"Never!" I said.

"Then don't let her go on a long journey this summer. She's not yet strong enough. And stop her smoking those vile black cigars."

In the end, the doctor had his way about the holiday, but not about the cigars. Rooms were booked for us in a place called the Hotel Magnificent in the famous seaside town of Bournemouth. Bournemouth, my grandmother told me, was full of old people like herself. They retired there by the thousand because the air was so bracing and healthy it kept them, so they believed, alive for a few extra years.

"Does it?" I asked.

"Of course not," she said. "It's tommyrot. But just for once I think we've got to obey the doctor."

Soon after that, my grandmother and I took the train to Bournemouth and settled into the Hotel Magnificent. It was an enormous white building on the sea-front and it looked to me like a pretty boring place to spend a summer holiday in. I had my own separate bedroom, but there was a door connecting my room with my grandmother's room so that we could visit each other without going into the corridor.

Just before we left for Bournemouth, my grandmother had given me, as consolation, a present of

two white mice in a little cage
and of course I took them with
me. They were terrific fun, those
mice. I called them William
and Mary, and in the hotel I set
out right away teaching them to
do tricks. The first trick I taught
them was to creep
up the sleeve of
my jacket and
come out by
my neck.

Then I taught them to climb up
the back of my neck on to the
top of my head. I did this by
putting cake crumbs in my hair.

On the very first morning after our arrival, the
chambermaid was making my bed when one of my
mice poked its head out from under the sheets.
The maid let out a shriek that brought a dozen
people running to see who was being murdered. I
was reported to the Manager. There followed an
unpleasant scene in the Manager's office with the
Manager, my grandmother and me.

The Manager, whose name was Mr Stringer, was
a bristly man in a black tail-coat. "I cannot permit
mice in my hotel, madam," he said to my grandmother.

"How dare you say that when your rotten hotel
is full of rats anyway!" my grandmother cried.

"Rats!" cried Mr Stringer, going mauve in the
face. "There are no rats in this hotel!"

"I saw one this very morning," my grandmother said. "It was running down the corridor into the kitchen!"

"That is not true!" cried Mr Stringer.

"You had better get the rat-catcher in at once," my grandmother said, "before I report you to the Public Health Authorities. I expect there's rats scuttling all over the kitchen floor and stealing the food off the shelves and jumping in and out of the soup!"

"Never!" cried Mr Stringer.

"No wonder my breakfast toast was all nibbled round the edges this morning," my grandmother went on relentlessly. "No wonder it had a nasty ratty taste. If you're not careful, the Health people will be ordering the entire hotel to be closed before everyone gets typhoid fever."

"You are not being serious, madam," Mr Stringer said.

"I was never more serious in my life," my grandmother said. "Are you or are you not going to allow my grandson to keep his white mice in his room?"

The Manager knew when he was beaten. "May I suggest a compromise, madam?" he said. "I will permit him to keep them in his room as long as they are never allowed out of the cage. How's that?"

"That will suit us very well," my grandmother said, and she stood up and marched out of the room with me behind her.

There is no way you can train mice inside a cage. Yet I dared not let them out because the chambermaid was spying on me all the time. She had a key to my door and she kept bursting in at all hours, trying to catch me with the mice out of the cage. She told me that the first mouse to break the rules would be drowned in a bucket of water by the hall-porter.

I decided to seek a safer place where I could

carry on with the training. There must surely be an empty room in this enormous hotel. I put one mouse into each trouser-pocket and wandered downstairs in search of a secret spot.

The ground floor of the hotel was a maze of public rooms, all of them named in gold letters on the doors. I wandered through "The Lounge" and "The Smoking-Room" and "The Card-Room" and "The Reading-Room" and "The Drawing-Room". None of them was empty. I went down a long wide corridor and at the end of it I came to 'The Ballroom'. There were double-doors leading into it, and in front of the doors there was a large notice-board on a stand. The notice on the board said,

RSPCC MEETING

STRICTLY PRIVATE
THIS ROOM IS RESERVED
FOR THE
ANNUAL MEETING
OF
THE ROYAL SOCIETY
FOR THE PREVENTION
OF CRUELTY TO CHILDREN

The double-doors into the room were open. I peeped in. It was a colossal room. There were rows and rows of chairs, all facing a platform. The chairs were painted gold and they had little red cushions on the seats. But there was not a soul in sight.

I sidled cautiously into the room. What a lovely secret silent place it was. The meeting of the Royal Society for the Prevention of Cruelty to Children must have taken place earlier in the day, and now they had all gone home. Even if they hadn't, even if they *did* suddenly come pouring in, they would be wonderful kind people who would look with favour upon a young mouse-trainer going about his business.

At the back of the room there was a large folding screen with Chinese dragons painted on it. I decided, just to be on the safe side, to go behind this screen and do my training there. I wasn't a bit frightened of the Prevention of Cruelty to Children people, but there was always a chance that Mr Stringer, the Manager, might pop his head round the door. If he did and if he saw the mice, the poor things would be in the hall-porter's bucket of water before I could shout stop.

I tiptoed to the back of the room and settled myself on the thick green carpet behind the big screen. What a splendid place this was! Ideal for mouse-training! I took William and Mary out of my trouser-pockets. They sat beside me on the carpet, quiet and well-behaved.

The trick I was going to teach them today was tight-rope walking. It is not all that difficult to train an intelligent mouse to be an expert tight-rope walker provided you know exactly how to go about it. First, you must have a piece of string. I had that. Then you must have some good cake. A fine currant cake is the favourite food of white mice. They are dotty about it. I had brought with me a rock cake which I had pocketed while having tea with Grandmamma the day before.

Now here's what you do. You stretch the string tight between your two hands, but you start by keeping it very short, only about three inches. You put the mouse on your right hand and a little piece of cake on your left hand. The mouse is therefore only three inches away from the cake. He can see it and he can smell it. His whiskers twitch with excitement. He can almost reach the cake by leaning forward, but not quite. He only has to take two steps along the string to reach this tasty morsel. He ventures forward, one paw on the string, then the other. If the mouse has a good sense of balance, and most of them have, he will get across easily. I started with William. He walked the string without a moment's hesitation. I let him have a quick nibble of the cake just to whet his appetite. Then I put him back on my right hand.

This time I lengthened the string. I made it about six inches long. William knew what to do now. With superb balance, he walked step by step along the string until he reached the cake. He was rewarded with another nibble.

Quite soon, William was walking a twenty-four-inch tight-rope (or rather tight-string) from one hand to the other to reach the cake. It was wonderful to watch him. He was enjoying himself tremendously. I was careful to hold the string near the carpet so that if he did lose his balance, he wouldn't have far to fall. But he never fell. William was obviously a natural acrobat, a great tight-rope-walking mouse.

Now it was Mary's turn. I put William on the carpet beside me and rewarded him with some extra crumbs and a currant. Then I started going through the same routine all over again with Mary. My blinding ambition, you see, my dream of dreams, was to become one day the owner of a White Mouse Circus. I would have a small stage with red curtains in front of it, and when the curtains were drawn apart, the audience would see my world-famous performing mice walking on tight-ropes, swinging from trapezes, turning somersaults in the air, bouncing on trampolines and all the rest of it. I would have white mice riding on white rats, and the rats would gallop furiously round and round the stage. I was beginning to picture myself travelling first-class all over the globe with my Famous White Mouse Circus, and performing before all the crowned heads of Europe.

I was about halfway through Mary's training when suddenly I heard voices outside the Ballroom door. The sound grew louder. It swelled into a great babble of speech from many throats. I recognised the voice of the awful Hotel Manager, Mr Stringer.

Help, I thought.

But thank heavens for the huge screen.

I crouched behind it and peered through the crack between two of the folding sections. I could see the entire length and width of the Ballroom without anyone seeing me.

"Well, ladies, I am sure you will be quite comfortable in here," Mr Stringer's voice was saying. Then in through the double-doors he marched, black tail-coat and all, spreading his arms wide as he ushered in a great flock of ladies. "If there is anything we can do for you, do not hesitate to let me know," he went on. "Tea will be served for all of you on the Sunshine Terrace after you have concluded your meeting." With that, he bowed and scraped himself out of the room as a vast herd of ladies from the Royal Society for the Prevention of Cruelty to Children came streaming in. They wore pretty clothes and all of them had hats on their heads.

The Meeting

Now that the Manager had gone, I was not particularly alarmed. What better than to be imprisoned in a room full of these splendid ladies? If I ever got talking to them, I might even suggest that they come and do a bit of cruelty-to-children preventing at my school. We could certainly use them there.

In they came, talking their heads off. They began milling round and choosing their seats, and there was a whole lot of stuff like, "Come and sit next to me, Millie dear," and "Oh, hel-*lo* Beatrice! I haven't seen you since the last meeting! What an adorable dress you have on!"

I decided to stay where I was and let them get on with their meeting while I got on with my mouse-training, but I watched them for a while longer through the crack in the screen, waiting for them to settle down. How many were there? I guessed about two hundred. The back rows filled up first. They all seemed to want to sit as far back from the platform as possible.

There was a lady wearing a tiny green hat in the middle of the back row who kept scratching the nape of her neck. She couldn't leave it alone. It fascinated me the way her fingers kept scratching away at the hair on the back of her neck. Had she known somebody was watching her from behind, I'm sure she would have been embarrassed. I wondered if she had dandruff. All of a sudden, I noticed that the lady next to her was doing the same thing!

And the next one!

And the next!

The whole lot of them were doing it. They were all scratching away like mad at the hair on the backs of their necks!

Did they have fleas in their hair?

More likely it was nits.

A boy at school called Ashton had had nits in his hair last term and the matron had made him dip his whole head in turpentine. It killed the nits all right, but it nearly killed Ashton as well. Half the skin came away from his scalp.

I began to be fascinated by these hair-scratching ladies. It is always funny when you catch someone doing something coarse and she thinks no one is looking. Nose-picking, for example, or scratching her bottom. Hair-scratching is very nearly as unattractive, especially if it goes on and on.

I decided it had to be nits.

Then the most astonishing thing happened. I saw one lady pushing her fingers up *underneath* the hair on her head, and the hair, *the entire head of hair* lifted upwards all in one piece, and the hand slid underneath the hair and went on scratching!

She was wearing a wig! She was also wearing gloves! I glanced swiftly around at the rest of the now seated audience. *Every one of them was wearing gloves!*

My blood turned to ice. I began to shake all over. I glanced frantically behind me for a back door to escape through. There wasn't one.

Should I leap out from behind the screen and make a dash for the double-doors?

Those double-doors were already closed and I could see a woman standing in front of them. She was bending forward and fixing some sort of a metal chain round the two door-handles.

Keep still, I told myself. No one has seen you yet. There's no reason in the world why they should come and look behind the screen. But one false move, one cough, one sneeze, one nose-blow, one little sound of any sort and it won't be just one witch that gets you. It'll be two hundred!

67

At that point, I think I fainted. The whole thing was altogether too much for a small boy to cope with. But I don't believe I was out for more than a few seconds, and when I came to, I was lying on the carpet and I was still, thank heavens, behind the screen. There was absolute silence all around me.

Rather shakily, I got to my knees and peered once again through the crack in the screen.

Frizzled Like a Fritter

All the women, or rather the witches, were now sitting motionless in their chairs and staring as though hypnotised at somebody who had suddenly appeared on the platform. That somebody was another woman.

The first thing I noticed about this woman was her size. She was tiny, probably no more than four and a half feet tall. She looked quite young, I guessed about twenty-five or six, and she was very pretty. She had on a rather stylish long black dress that reached right to the ground and she wore black gloves that came up to her elbows. Unlike the others, she wasn't wearing a hat.

She didn't look to me like a witch at all, but she couldn't possibly *not* be one, otherwise what on earth was she doing up there on the platform? And why, for heaven's sake, were all the other witches gazing at her with such a mixture of adoration, awe and fear?

Very slowly, the young lady on the platform raised her hands to her face. I saw her gloved fingers unhooking something behind her ears, and then . . . then she caught hold of her cheeks and lifted her face clean away! The whole of that pretty face came away in her hands!

It was a mask!

As she took off the mask, she turned sideways and placed it carefully upon a small table near by, and when she turned round again and faced us, I very nearly screamed out loud.

That face of hers was the most frightful and frightening thing I have ever seen. Just looking at it gave me the shakes all over. It was so crumpled and wizened, so shrunken and shrivelled, it looked as though it had been pickled in vinegar. It was a fearsome and ghastly sight. There was something terribly wrong with it, something foul and putrid and decayed. It seemed quite literally to be rotting away at the edges, and in the middle of the face, around the mouth and cheeks, I could see the skin all cankered and worm-eaten, as though maggots were working away in there.

There are times when something is so frightful you become mesmerised by it and can't look away. I was like that now. I was transfixed. I was numbed. I was magnetised by the sheer horror of this woman's features. But there was more to it than that. There was a look of serpents in those eyes of hers as they flashed around the audience.

I knew immediately, of course, that this was none other than The Grand High Witch herself. I knew also why she had worn a mask. She could never have moved around in public, let alone book in at an hotel, with her real face. Everyone who saw her would have run away screaming.

"The doors!" shouted The Grand High Witch in a voice that filled the room and bounced around the walls. "Are they chained and bolted?"

"The doors are chained and bolted, Your Grandness," answered a voice in the audience.

The brilliant snake's eyes that were set so deep in that dreadful rotting worm-eaten face glared unblinkingly at the witches who sat facing her. "You may rrree-moof your gloves!" she shouted.

Her voice, I noticed, had that same hard metallic quality as the voice of the witch I had met under the conker tree, only it was far louder and much much harsher. It rasped. It grated. It snarled. It scraped. It shrieked. And it growled.

Everyone in the room was peeling off her gloves. I was watching the hands of those in the back row. I wanted very much to see what their fingers looked like and whether my grandmother had been right. Ah! . . . Yes! . . . I could see several of them now! I could see the brown claws curving over the tips of the fingers! They were about two inches long, those claws, and sharp at the ends!

"You may rrree-moof your shoes!" barked The Grand High Witch.

I heard a sigh of relief going up from all the witches in the room as they kicked off their narrow high-heeled shoes, and then I got a glimpse under the chairs of several pairs of stockinged feet, square and completely toeless. Revolting they were, as though the toes had been sliced away from the feet with a carving-knife.

"You may rrree-moof your vigs!" snarled The Grand High Witch. She had a peculiar way of speaking. There was some sort of a foreign accent there, something harsh and guttural, and she seemed to have trouble pronouncing the letter w. As well as that, she did something funny with the letter r. She would roll it round and round her mouth like a piece of hot pork-crackling before spitting it out. "Rrree-moof your vigs and get some fresh air into your spotty scalps!" she shouted, and another sigh of relief arose from the audience as all the hands went up to the heads and all the wigs (with the hats still on them) were lifted away.

There now appeared in front of me row upon row of bald female heads, a sea of naked scalps, every one of them red and itchy-looking from being rubbed by the linings of the wigs. I simply cannot tell you how awful they were, and somehow the whole sight was made more grotesque because underneath those frightful scabby bald heads, the bodies were dressed in fashionable and rather pretty clothes. It was monstrous. It was unnatural.

Oh heavens, I thought. Oh help! Oh Lord have mercy on me! These foul bald-headed females are child-killers every one of them, and here I am imprisoned in the same room and I can't escape!

At that point, a new and doubly horrifying thought struck me. My grandmother had said that

with their special nose-holes they could smell out
a child on a pitch-black night from right across the
other side of the road. Up to now, my grandmother
had been right every time. It seemed a certainty
therefore that one of the witches in the back row
was going to sniff me out at any moment and then
the yell of "Dogs' droppings!" would go up all over
the room and I would be cornered like a rat.

I knelt on the carpet behind the screen, hardly
daring to breathe.

Then suddenly I remembered another very
important thing my grandmother had told me.
"The dirtier you are," she had said, "the harder it
is for a witch to smell you out."

How long since I had last had a bath?

Not for ages. I had my own room in the hotel
and my grandmother never bothered with silly
things like that. Come to think of it, I don't
believe I'd had a bath since we arrived.

When had I last washed my hands or face?

75

Certainly not this morning.

Not yesterday either.

I glanced down at my hands. They were covered with smudge and mud and goodness knows what else besides.

So perhaps I had a chance after all. The stink-waves couldn't possibly get out through all that dirt.

"Vitches of Inkland!" shouted The Grand High Witch. She herself I noticed had not taken off either her wig or her gloves or her shoes. "Vitches of Inkland!" she yelled.

The audience stirred uneasily and sat up straighter in their chairs.

"Miserrrable vitches!" she yelled. "Useless lazy vitches! Feeble frrribbling vitches! You are a heap of idle good-for-nothing vurms!"

A shudder went through the audience. The Grand High Witch was clearly in an ugly mood and they knew it. I had a feeling that something awful was going to happen soon.

"I am having my breakfast this morning," cried The Grand High Witch, "and I am looking out of the vindow at the beach, and vot am I seeing? I am asking you, *vot am I seeing?* I am seeing a rrree-volting sight! I am seeing hundreds, I am seeing *thousands* of rrrotten rrree-pulsive little children playing on the sand! It is putting me rrright off my food! *Vye have you not got rrrid of them?*" she screamed. "Vye have you not rrrubbed them all out, these filthy smelly children?"

With each word she spoke, flecks of pale-blue

76

phlegm shot from her mouth like little bullets.

"I am asking you *vye!*" she screamed.

Nobody answered her question.

"Children smell!" she screamed. "They stink out the vurld! Vee do not vont these children around here!"

The bald heads in the audience all nodded vigorously.

"Vun child a veek is no good to me!" The Grand High Witch cried out. "Is that the best you can do?"

"We will do better," murmured the audience. "We will do much better."

"Better is no good either!" shrieked The Grand High Witch. "I demand maximum rrree-sults! So here are my orders! My orders are that every single child in this country shall be rrrubbed out, sqvashed, sqvirted, sqvittered and frrrittered before I come here again in vun year's time! Do I make myself clear?"

A great gasp went up from the audience. I saw the witches all looking at one another with deeply troubled expressions. And I heard one witch at the end of the front row saying aloud, "*All* of them! We can't possibly wipe out *all* of them!"

The Grand High Witch whipped round as though someone had stuck a skewer into her bottom. "Who said that?" she snapped. "Who dares to argue vith me? It vos you, vos it not?" She pointed a gloved finger as sharp as a needle at the witch who had spoken.

"I didn't mean it, Your Grandness!" the witch

cried out. "I didn't mean to argue! I was just talking to myself!"

"You dared to argue vith me!" screamed The Grand High Witch.

"I was just talking to myself!" cried the wretched witch. "I swear it, Your Grandness!" She began to shake with fear.

The Grand High Witch took a quick step forward, and when she spoke again, it was in a voice that made my blood run cold.

"A stupid vitch who answers back
Must burn until her bones are black!"

she screamed.

"No, no!" begged the witch in the front row. The Grand High Witch went on,

"A foolish vitch vithout a brain
Must sizzle in the fiery flame!"

"Save me!" cried the wretched witch in the front row. The Grand High Witch took no notice of her. She spoke again.

"An idiotic vitch like you
Must rrroast upon the barbecue!"

"Forgive me, O Your Grandness!" cried the miserable culprit. "I didn't mean it!" But The Grand
High Witch continued with her terrible recital.

"A vitch who dares to say I'm wrrrong
Vill not be vith us very long!"

A moment later, a stream of sparks that looked
like tiny white-hot metal-filings came shooting
out of The Grand High Witch's eyes and flew
straight towards the one who had dared to speak. I
saw the sparks striking against her and burrowing
into her and she screamed a horrible howling
scream and a puff of smoke rose up around her. A
smell of burning meat filled the room.

Nobody moved. Like me, they were all watching

the smoke, and when it had cleared away, the chair was empty. I caught a glimpse of something wispy-white, like a little cloud, fluttering upwards and disappearing out of the window.

A great sigh rose up from the audience.

The Grand High Witch glared around the room. "I hope nobody else is going to make me cross today," she remarked.

There was a deathly silence.

"Frrrizzled like a frrritter," said The Grand High Witch. "Cooked like a carrot. You vill never see *her* again. Now vee can get down to business."

Formula 86 Delayed Action Mouse-Maker

"Children are rrree-volting!" screamed The Grand High Witch. "Vee vill vipe them all avay! Vee vill scrrrub them off the face of the earth! Vee vill flush them down the drain!"

"Yes, yes!" chanted the audience. "Wipe them away! Scrub them off the earth! Flush them down the drain!"

"Children are foul and filthy!" thundered The Grand High Witch.

"They are! They are!" chorused the English witches. "They are foul and filthy!"

"Children are dirty and stinky!" screamed The Grand High Witch.

"Dirty and stinky!" cried the audience, getting more and more worked up.

"Children are smelling of *dogs' drrroppings*!" screeched The Grand High Witch.

"Pooooooo!" cried the audience. "Pooooooo! Pooooooo! Pooooooo!"

"They are vurse than dogs' drrroppings!" screeched The Grand High Witch. "Dogs' drrroppings is smelling like violets and prrrimroses compared vith children!"

"Violets and primroses!" chanted the audience. They were clapping and cheering almost every word spoken from the platform. The speaker seemed to have them completely under her spell.

"To talk about children is making me sick!" screamed The Grand High Witch. "I am feeling sick even *thinking* about them! Fetch me a basin!"

The Grand High Witch paused and glared at the mass of eager faces in the audience. They waited, wanting more.

"So now!" barked The Grand High Witch. "So now I am having a plan! I am having a giganticus plan for getting rrrid of every single child in the whole of Inkland!"

The witches gasped. They gaped. They turned and gave each other ghoulish grins of excitement.

"Yes!" thundered The Grand High Witch. "Vee shall svish them and svollop them and vee shall make to disappear every single smelly little brrrat in Inkland in vun strrroke!"

"Whoopee!" cried the witches, clapping their hands. "You are brilliant, O Your Grandness! You are fantabulous!"

"Shut up and listen!" snapped The Grand High Witch. "Listen very carefully and let us not be having any muck-ups!"

The audience leaned forward, eager to learn how this magic was going to be performed.

"Each and every vun of you", thundered The Grand High Witch, "is to go back to your home towns immediately and rrree-sign from your jobs. Rrree-sign! Give notice! Rrree-tire!"

"We will!" they cried. "We will resign from our jobs!"

"And after you have rrree-signed from your

jobs," The Grand High Witch went on, "each and every vun of you vill be going out and you vill be buying . . . " She paused.

"What will we be buying?" they cried. "Tell us, O Brilliant One, what is it we shall be buying?"

"Sveet-shops!" shouted The Grand High Witch.

"Sweet-shops!" they cried. "We are going to buy sweet-shops! What a frumptious wheeze!"

"Each of you vill be buying for herself a sveet-shop. You vill be buying the very best and most rrree-spectable sveet-shops in Inkland."

"We will! We will!" they answered. Their dreadful voices were like a chorus of dentists' drills all grinding away together.

"I am vonting no tuppenny-ha'penny crrrummy little tobacco-selling-newspaper-sveet-shops!" shouted The Grand High Witch. "I am vonting you to get only the very best shops filled up high vith piles and piles of luscious sveets and tasty chocs!"

"The best!" they cried. "We shall buy the best sweet-shops in town!"

"You vill be having no trouble in getting vot you vont," shouted The Grand High Witch, "because you vill be offering four times as much as a shop is vurth and nobody is rrree-fusing an offer like that! Money is not a prrroblem to us vitches as you know very vell. I have brrrought vith me six trrrunks stuffed full of Inklish banknotes, all new and crrrisp. And all of them," she added with a fiendish leer, "all of them homemade."

The witches in the audience grinned, appreciating this joke.

At that point, one foolish witch got so excited at the possibilities presented by owning a sweet-shop that she leapt to her feet and shouted, "The children will come flocking to my shop and I will feed them poisoned sweets and poisoned chocs and wipe them all out like weasels!"

The room became suddenly silent. I saw the tiny body of The Grand High Witch stiffen and then go rigid with rage. "Who spoke?" she shrieked. "It vos *you!* You over there!"

The culprit sat down fast and covered her face with her clawed hands.

"You blithering bumpkin!" screeched The Grand High Witch. "You brrrainless bogvumper! Are you not rrree-alising that if you are going rrround poisoning little children you vill be caught in five minutes flat? Never in my life am I hearing such a boshvolloping suggestion coming from a vitch!"

The entire audience cowered and shook. I'm quite sure they all thought, as I did, that the terrible white-hot sparks were about to start flying again.

Curiously enough, they didn't.

'If such a tomfiddling idea is all you can be coming up vith," thundered The Grand High Witch, "then it is no vunder Inkland is still svorming vith rrrotten little children!"

There was another silence. The Grand High Witch glared at the witches in the audience. "Do you not know", she shouted at them, "that vee vitches are vurrrking only vith magic?"

"We know, Your Grandness!" they all answered. "Of course we know!"

The Grand High Witch grated her bony gloved hands against each other and cried out, "So each of you is owning a magnificent sveet-shop! The next move is that each of you vill be announcing in the vindow of your shop that on a certain day you vill be having a Great Gala Opening vith frree sveets and chocs to every child!"

"That will bring them in, the greedy little brutes!" cried the audience. "They'll be fighting to get through the doors!"

"Next," continued The Grand High Witch, "you vill prepare yourselves for this Great Gala Opening by filling every choc and every sveet in your shop vith my very latest and grrreatest magic

85

formula! This is known as FORMULA 86 DELAYED ACTION MOUSE-MAKER!"

"Delayed Action Mouse-Maker!" they chanted. "She's done it again! Her Grandness has concocted yet another of her wondrous magic child-killers! How do we make it, O Brilliant One?"

"Exercise patience," answered The Grand High Witch. "First, I am explaining to you how my Formula 86 Delayed Action Mouse-Maker is vurrrking. Listen carefully."

"We are listening!" cried the audience who were now jumping up and down in their chairs with excitement.

"Delayed Action Mouse-Maker is a green liqvid," explained The Grand High Witch, "and vun droplet in each choc or sveet vill be qvite enough. So here is vot happens:

"Child eats choc vich has in it Delayed Action Mouse-Maker liqvid . . .

"Child goes home feeling fine . . .

"Child goes to bed, still feeling fine . . .

"Child vakes up in the morning still okay . . .

"Child goes to school still feeling fine . . .

"Formula, you understand, is *delayed action*, and is not vurrrking yet."

"We understand, O Brainy One!" cried the audience. "But when does it start working?"

"It is starting to vurrrk at exactly nine o'clock, vhen the child is arriving at school!" shouted The Grand High Witch triumphantly. "Child arrives at school. Delayed Action Mouse-Maker immediately starts to vurrrk. Child starts to

86

shrrrink. Child is starting to grow fur. Child is starting to grow tail. All is happening in prrreecisely twenty-six seconds. After twenty-six seconds, child is not a child any longer. It is a mouse!"

"A mouse!" cried the witches. "What a frumptious thought!"

"Classrooms vill all be svorrrming vith mice!" shouted The Grand High Witch. "Chaos and pandemonium vill be rrreigning in every school in Inkland! Teachers vill be hopping up and down! Vimmen teachers vill be standing on desks and holding up skirts and yelling, 'Help, help, help!'"

"They will! They will!" cried the audience.

"And vot", shouted The Grand High Witch, "is happening next in every school?"

"Tell us!" they cried. "Tell us, O Brainy One!"

The Grand High Witch stretched her stringy neck forward and grinned at the audience, showing two rows of pointed teeth, slightly blue. She raised her voice louder than ever and shouted, *"Mouse-trrraps is coming out!"*

"Mouse-traps!" cried the witches.

"And cheese!" shouted The Grand High Witch. "Teachers is all rrrushing and rrrunning out and getting mouse-trrraps and baiting them vith cheese and putting them down all over school! Mice is nibbling cheese! Mouse-trrraps is going off! All over school, mouse-trrraps is going *snappety-snap* and mouse-heads is rrrolling across the floors like marbles! All over Inkland, in everrry school in Inkland, noise of snapping mouse-trrraps vill be heard!"

At this point, the disgusting old Grand High Witch began to do a sort of witch's dance up and down the platform, stamping her feet and clapping her hands. The entire audience joined in the clapping and the foot-stamping. They were making such a tremendous racket that I thought surely

Mr Stringer would hear it and come banging at the door. But he didn't.

Then, above all the noise, I heard the voice of The Grand High Witch screaming out some sort of an awful gloating song,

"Down vith children! Do them in!
Boil their bones and fry their skin!
Bish them, sqvish them, bash them, mash
    them!
Brrreak them, shake them, slash them, smash
    them!
Offer chocs vith magic powder!
Say 'Eat up!' then say it louder.
Crrram them full of sticky eats,
Send them home still guzzling sveets.
And in the morning little fools
Go marching off to separate schools.
A girl feels sick and goes all pale.
She yells, 'Hey look! I've grrrown a tail!'
A boy who's standing next to her
Screams, 'Help! I think I'm grrrowing fur!'
Another shouts, 'Vee look like frrreaks!
There's viskers growing on our cheeks!'
A boy who vos extremely tall
Cries out, 'Vot's wrong? I'm grrrowing small!'
Four tiny legs begin to sprrrout
From everybody rrround about.
And all at vunce, all in a trrrice,
There are no children! Only MICE!
In every school is mice galore
All rrrunning rrround the school-rrroom floor!

And all the poor demented teachers
Is yelling, 'Hey, who are these crrreatures?'
They stand upon the desks and shout,
'Get out, you filthy mice! Get out!
Vill someone fetch some mouse-trrraps,
    please!
And don't forrrget to bring the cheese!'
Now mouse-trrraps come and every trrrap
Goes *snippy-snip* and *snappy-snap*.
The mouse-trrraps have a powerful spring,
The springs go *crack* and *snap* and *ping*!
Is lovely noise for us to hear!

Is music to a vitch's ear!
Dead mice is every place arrround,
Piled two feet deep upon the grrround,
Vith teachers searching left and rrright,
But not a single child in sight!
The teachers cry, 'Vot's going on?
Oh vhere have all the children gone?
Is half-past nine and as a rrrule
They're never late as this for school!'
Poor teachers don't know vot to do.
Some sit and rrread, and just a few
Amuse themselves throughout the day
By sveeping all the mice avay.
AND ALL US VITCHES SHOUT HOORAY!"

The Recipe

I hope you haven't forgotten that while all this was going on I was still stuck behind the screen on my hands and knees with one eye glued to the crack. I don't know how long I had been there but it seemed like for ever. The worst part of it was not being allowed to cough or make a sound, and knowing that if I did, I was as good as dead. And all the way through, I was living in constant terror that one of the witches in the back row was going to get a whiff of my presence through those special nose-holes of hers.

My only hope, as I saw it, was the fact that I hadn't washed for days. That and the never-ending excitement and clapping and shouting that was going on in the room. The witches were thinking of nothing except The Grand High Witch up there on the platform and her great plan for wiping out all the children of England. They certainly weren't sniffing around for a child in the room. In their wildest dreams (if witches have dreams), that would never have occurred to any of them. I kept still and prayed.

The Grand High Witch's dreadful gloating song was over now, and the audience was clapping madly and shouting, "Brilliant! Sensational! Marvellous! You are a genius, O Brainy One! It is a thrilling invention, this Delayed Action Mouse-Maker! It is a winner! And the beauty of it is that the teachers will be the ones who bump off the stinking little children! It won't be us doing it! We shall never be caught!"

"Vitches are never caught!" snapped The Grand High Witch. "Attention now! I vont everybody's attention for I am about to be telling you vot you must do to prepare Formula 86 Delayed Action Mouse-Maker!"

Suddenly there came a great gasp from the audience. This was followed by a hubbub of shrieking and yelling, and I saw many of the witches leaping to their feet and pointing at the platform and crying out, "Mice! Mice! Mice! She's done it to show us! The Brainy One has turned two children into mice and there they are!"

I looked toward the platform. The mice were there all right, two of them, running around near The Grand High Witch's skirts.

But these were not field mice or house mice or wood mice or harvest mice. They were *white mice!* I recognised them immediately as being my own little William and Mary!

"Mice!" shouted the audience. "Our leader has made mice to appear out of nowhere! Get the mouse-traps! Fetch the cheese!"

I saw The Grand High Witch peering down at the floor and staring with obvious puzzlement at William and Mary. She bent lower to get a closer look. Then she straightened up and shouted, "Qviet!"

The audience became silent and sat down.

"These mice are nothing to do vith me!" she shouted. "These mice are *pet* mice! These mice are qvite obviously belonging to some rrreepellent little child in the hotel! A boy it vill be for a certainty because girls are not keeping pet mice!"

"A boy!" cried the witches. "A filthy smelly little boy! We'll swipe him! We'll swizzle him! We'll have his tripes for breakfast!"

"Silence!" shouted The Grand High Witch, raising her hands. "You know perrrfectly vell you must do nothing to drrraw attention to yourselves vhile you are living in the hotel! Let us by all means get rrrid of this evil-smelling little sqvirt, but vee must do it as qvietly as possible, for are vee not all of us the most rrree-spectable ladies of the Rrroyal Society for the Prrree-vention of Crrruelty to Children?"

"What do you suggest then, O Brainy One?" they cried out. "How shall we dispose of this small pile of filth?"

They're talking about me, I thought. These females are actually talking about how to kill me. I began to sweat.

"Whoever he is, he is not important," announced The Grand High Witch. "Leave him to me. I shall smell him out and turn him into a mackerel and have him dished up for supper."

"Bravo!" cried the witches. "Cut off his head and chop off his tail and fry him in hot butter!"

You can imagine that none of this was making

94

me feel very comfortable. William and Mary were still running around on the platform, and I saw The Grand High Witch aim a swift running kick at William. She caught him right on the point of her toe and sent him flying. She did the same to Mary. Her aim was extraordinary. She would have made a great football player. Both mice crashed against the wall, and for a few moments they lay stunned. Then they got to their feet and scampered away.

"Attention again!" The Grand High Witch was

shouting. "I vill now give to you the rrrecipe for
concocting Formula 86 Delayed Action Mouse-
Maker! Get out pencils and paper."

Handbags were opened all over the room and
notebooks were fished out.

"Give us the recipe, O Brainy One!" cried the
audience impatiently. "Tell us the secret."

"First," said The Grand High Witch, "I had to
find something that vould cause the children to
become very small very qvickly."

"And what was that?" cried the audience.

"That part vos simple," said The Grand High
Witch. "All you have to do if you are vishing to
make a child very small is to look at him through
the wrrrong end of a telescope."

"She's a wonder!" cried the audience. "Who else
would have thought of a thing like that?"

"So you take the wrrrong end of a telescope,"
continued The Grand High Witch, "and you boil it
until it gets soft."

"How long does that take?" they asked her.

"Tventy-vun hours of boiling," answered The
Grand High Witch. "And vhile this is going on,
you take exactly forty-five brrrown mice and you

96

chop off their tails vith a carving-knife and you fry
the tails in hair-oil until they are nice and crrrisp."

"What do we do with all those mice who have
had their tails chopped off?" asked the audience.

"You simmer them in frog-juice for vun hour,"
came the answer. "But listen to me. So far I have
only given you the easy part of the rrrecipe. The
rrreally difficult problem is to put in something
that vill have a genuine delayed action
rrree-sult, something that can be
eaten by children on a certain day
but vhich vill not start vurrrking
on them until nine o'clock the
next morning vhen they
arrive at school."

"What did you come up

with, O Brainy One?" they called out. "Tell us the great secret!"

"The secret", announced The Grand High Witch triumphantly, "is an *alarm-clock!*"

"An alarm-clock!" they cried. "It's a stroke of genius!"

"Of course it is," said The Grand High Witch. "You can set a tventy-four-hour alarm-clock today and at exactly nine o'clock tomorrow it vill go off."

"But we will need five million alarm-clocks!" cried the audience. "We will need one for each child!"

"Idiots!" shouted The Grand High Witch. "If you are vonting a steak, you do not cook the whole cow! It is the same vith alarm-clocks. Vun clock vill make enough for a thousand children. Here is vhat you do. You set your alarm-clock to go off at nine o'clock tomorrow morning. Then you rrroast it in the oven until it is crrrisp and tender. Are you wrrriting this down?"

"We are, Your Grandness, we are!" they cried.

"Next," said The Grand High Witch, "you take your boiled telescope and your frrried mouse-tails

and your cooked mice and your rrroasted alarm-clock and all together you put them into the mixer. Then you mix them at full speed. This vill give you a nice thick paste. Vhile the mixer is still mixing you must add to it the yolk of vun grrruntle's egg."

"A gruntle's egg!" cried the audience. "We shall do that!" Underneath all the clamour that was going on I heard one witch in the back row saying to her neighbour, "I'm getting a bit old to go bird's nesting. Those ruddy gruntles always nest very high up."

"So you mix in the egg,"

The Grand High Witch went on, "and vun after the other you also mix in the following items: the claw of a crrrabcrrruncher, the beak of a blabbersnitch, the snout of a grrrobblesqvirt and the tongue of a

catsprrringer. I trust you are not having any trrrouble finding those."

"None at all!" they cried out. "We will spear the blabbersnitch and trap the crabcruncher and shoot the grobblesquirt and catch the catspringer in his burrow!"

"Excellent!" said The Grand High Witch. "Vhen

99

you have mixed everything together in the mixer, you vill have a most marvellous-looking grrreen liqvid. Put vun drop, just vun titchy droplet of this liqvid into a chocolate or a sveet, and *at nine o'clock the next morning* the child who ate it vill turn into a mouse in tventy-six seconds! But vun vurd of vorning. Never increase the dose. Never put more than vun drrrop into each sveet or chocolate. And never give more than vun sweet or chocolate to each child. An overdose of Delayed Action Mouse-Maker vill mess up the timing of the alarm-clock and cause the child to turn into a mouse too early. A large overdose might even have an instant effect, and you vouldn't vont that, vould you? You vouldn't vont the children turning into mice rrright there in your sveet-shops. That vould give the game away. So be very carrreful! Do not overdose!"

Bruno Jenkins Disappears

The Grand High Witch was starting to talk again. "I am now going to prrrove to you", she said, "that this rrrecipe is vurrrking to perrrfection. You understand, of course, that you can set the alarm-clock to go off at any time you like. It does not *have* to be nine o'clock. So yesterday I am personally prrree-paring a small qvantity of the magic formula in order to give to you a public demonstration. But I am making vun small change in the rrrecipe. Before I am rrroasting the alarm-clock, I am setting it to go off, not at nine o'clock the next morning, but at half-past thrrree the next afternoon. Vhich means half-past thrrree *this* afternoon. And that", she said, glancing at her wrist-watch, "is in prrree-cisely seven minutes' time!"

The audience of witches was listening intently, sensing that something dramatic was about to happen.

"So vot am I doing yesterday vith this magic liqvid?" asked The Grand High Witch. "I vill tell you vot I am doing. I am putting vun drrroplet of it into a very sqvishy chocolate bar and I am giving this bar to a rrree-pulsive smelly little boy who is hanging rrround the lobby of the hotel."

The Grand High Witch paused. The audience

remained silent, waiting for her to go on.

"I votched this rrree-pulsive little brrrute gobbling up the sqvishy bar of chocolate and vhen he had finished, I said to him, 'Vos that good?' He said it vos great. So I said to him, 'Vould you like some more?' And he said, 'Yes.' So I said, 'I vill give you *six* more chocolate bars like that if you vill meet me in the Ballroom of this hotel at tventy-five-past thrrree tomorrow afternoon.' 'Six bars!' cried this greedy little svine. 'I'll be there! You bet I'll be there!'

"So the stage is set!" shouted The Grand High Witch. "The prrroof of the pudding is about to begin! Do not forget that before I am rrroasting the alarm-clock yesterday, I am setting it for half-past thrrree today. It is now" – she glanced again at her watch – "it is now exactly tventy-five minutes past thrrree and the nasty little stinker who vill be turning into a mouse in five minutes' time should at this very moment be standing outside the doors!"

And by gum, she was absolutely right. The boy, whoever he might be, was already rattling the door-handle and banging on the doors with his fist.

"Qvick!" shrieked The Grand High Witch. "Put on your vigs! Put on your gloves! Put on your shoes!"

There was a great rustle and bustle of putting on wigs and gloves and shoes, and I saw The Grand High Witch herself reach for her face-mask and put it on over that revolting face of hers. It was astonishing how that mask transformed her. All of

102

a sudden she became once again a rather pretty young lady.

"Let me in!" came the boy's voice from behind the doors. "Where are those chocolate bars you promised me? I'm here to collect! Dish them out!"

"He is not only smelly, he is also grrreedy," said The Grand High Witch. "Rrree-moof the chains from the doors and let him come in." The extra-ordinary thing about the mask was that its lips moved quite naturally when she spoke. You really couldn't see it was a mask at all.

One of the witches leapt to her feet and unfastened the chains. She opened the two huge doors. Then I heard her saying, "Why *hello*, little man. How lovely to see you. You have come for your chocolate bars, have you not? They are all ready for you. Do come in."

A small boy wearing a white tee-shirt and grey shorts and gymshoes entered the room. I recognised him at once. He was called Bruno Jenkins and he was staying in the hotel with his parents. I didn't care for him. He was one of those boys who is always eating something whenever you meet him. Meet him in the hotel lobby and he is stuffing sponge cake into his mouth. Pass him in the corridor and he is fishing potato crisps out of a bag by the fistful. Catch sight of him in the hotel garden and he is wolfing a Dairy Milk Bar and has two more sticking out of his trouser-pocket. What's more, Bruno never stopped boasting about how his father made more money than my father and that they owned three cars. But worse than that, yesterday morning I had found him

103

kneeling on the flagstones of the hotel terrace with a magnifying-glass in his hand. There was a column of ants marching across one of the flagstones and Bruno Jenkins was focusing the sun through his magnifying-glass and roasting the ants one by one. "I like watching them burn," he said. "That's horrible!" I cried. "Stop doing it!" "Let's see you stop me," he said. At that point I had pushed him with all my might and he had crashed sideways on to the flagstones. His magnifying-glass had splintered into many pieces and he had leapt up shrieking, "My father is going to get you for this!" Then he had run off, presumably to find his wealthy dad. That was the last time I had seen Bruno Jenkins until now. I doubted very much that he was about to be turned into a mouse, although I must confess that I was secretly hoping it might happen. Either way, I didn't envy him being up there in front of all those witches.

"Darling boy," cooed The Grand High Witch from up on the platform. "I have your chocolates all rrready for you. Do come up here firrrst and say hello to all these lovely ladies." Her voice was quite different now. It was soft and gentle and absolutely dripping with syrup.

Bruno was looking a bit bewildered, but he allowed himself to be led up on to the platform, where he stood beside The Grand High Witch and said, "Okay, where are my six bars of chocolate?"

I saw the witch who had let him in quietly putting the chain back on the door-handles. Bruno didn't notice this. He was too busy asking for his chocolate.

"The time is now vun minute before half-past thrrree!" announced The Grand High Witch.

"What the heck's going on?" Bruno asked. He wasn't frightened, but he wasn't looking exactly comfortable either. "What *is* this?" he said. "Gimme my chocolate!"

"Thirty seconds to go!" cried The Grand High Witch, gripping Bruno by the arm. Bruno shook himself clear and stared at her. She stared back at him, smiling with the lips of her mask. Every witch in the audience was staring at Bruno.

"Tventy seconds!" cried The Grand High Witch.

"Gimme the chocolate!" shouted Bruno, becoming suddenly suspicious. "Gimme the chocolate and let me out of here!"

"Fifteen seconds!" cried The Grand High Witch.

"Will one of you crazy punks kindly tell me what all this is about?" shouted Bruno.

"Ten seconds!" cried The Grand High Witch.

"Nine . . . eight . . . seven . . . six . . . five . . . four . . . thrrree . . . two . . . vun . . . zero! Vee have ignition!"

I could have sworn I heard an alarm-clock ringing. I saw Bruno jump. He jumped as though someone had stuck a hatpin deep into his bottom and he yelled "Ow!" He jumped so high that he landed on a small table up there on the stage, and he started hopping about on the top of this table, waving his arms and yelling his head off. Then suddenly he became silent. His whole body stiffened.

"The alarm has gone off!" shrieked The Grand High Witch. "The Mouse-Maker is beginning to vurrrk!" She started hopping about on the platform and clapping her gloved hands together and then she shouted out,

"This smelly brrrat, this filthy scum
This horrid little louse
Vill very very soon become
A lovely little MOUSE!"

Bruno was getting smaller by the second. I could see him shrinking . . .
Now his clothes seemed to be disappearing and brown fur was growing all over his body . . .
Suddenly he had a tail . . .
And then he had whiskers . . .
Now he had four feet . . .
It was all happening so quickly . . .
It was a matter of seconds only . . .
And all at once he wasn't there any more . . .

107

A small brown mouse was running around on the table top . . .

"Bravo!" yelled the audience. "She's done it! It works! It's fantastic! It's colossal! It's the greatest yet! You are a miracle, O Brainy One!" They were all standing up and clapping and cheering and The Grand High Witch produced a mouse-trap from the folds of her dress and started to set it.

Oh no! I thought. I don't want to see this! Bruno Jenkins may have been a bit of a stinker but I'm dashed if I want to watch him having his head chopped off!

"Vhere is he?" snapped The Grand High Witch, searching the platform. "Vhere has that mouse got to?"

She couldn't find him. Clever Bruno must have jumped down off the table and scampered off into some corner or even down a small hole. Thank heavens for that.

"It matters not!" shouted The Grand High Witch. "Silence and sit down!"

The Ancient Ones

The Grand High Witch stood on the very centre of the platform, and those dangerous eyes of hers travelled slowly around the audience of witches who were sitting so meekly before her. "All those over seventy put up your hands!" she barked suddenly.

Seven or eight hands went up in the air.

"It comes to me", said The Grand High Witch, "that you ancient vuns vill not be able to climb high trrrees in search of grrruntles' eggs."

"We won't, Your Grandness! We are afraid we won't!" chanted the ancient ones.

"Nor vill you be able to catch the crrrabcrrruncher, who lives high up on rrrocky cliffs," The Grand High Witch went on. "I can't exactly see you sprrrinting after the speedy catsprrringer either, or diving into deep vorters to spear the blabbersnitch, or striding the bleak moors vith a gun under your arm to shoot the grrrobblesqvirt. You are too old and feeble for those things."

"We are," chanted the ancient ones. "We are! We are!"

"You ancient vuns have served me vell over many years," said The Grand High Witch, "and I do not vish to deny you the pleasure of bumping off a few thousand children each just because you

110

have become old and feeble. I have therefore prepared personally vith my own hands a limited
qvantity of Delayed Action Mouse-Maker vhich I
vill distrrribute to the ancient vuns before you
leave the hotel."

"Oh, thank you, thank you!" cried the old
witches. "You are far too good to us, Your Grandness! You are so kind and thoughtful!"

"Here is a sample of vot I am giving you,"
shouted The Grand High Witch. She fished around
in a pocket of her dress and brought out a very

small bottle. She held it up and shouted, "In this tiny bottle is five hundred doses of Mouse-Maker! Is enough to turrrn five hundred children into mice!" I could see that the bottle was made of dark-blue glass and that it was very small, about the same size as the ones you can buy at the chemist with nose-drops in them. "Each of you ancient vuns vill get two of these bottles!" she shouted.

"Thank you, thank you, O Most Generous and Thoughtful One!" chorused the ancient witches. "Not one drop will be wasted! Each of us will promise to squish and squallop and squiggle one thousand children!"

"Our meeting is over!" announced The Grand High Witch. "Here is the time-table for the rrree-mainder of your stay in this hotel.

"Rrright now, vee must all go out on to the Sunshine Terrace and have tea vith that rrridiculous Manager.

"Next, at six o'clock tonight, those vitches who are too old to climb trees after grrruntles' eggs vill rrree-port to my rrroom to rrree-ceive two bottles each of Mouse-Maker. My rrroom number is 454. Do not forget it.

"Then, at eight o'clock, all of you vill assemble in the Dining-Rrroom for supper. Vee are the lovely ladies of the RSPCC and they are setting up two long tables specially for us. But do not forget to put the cotton plugs up your noses. That Dining-Rrroom vill be full of filthy little children and vithout the nose-plugs the stink vill be unbearrrable. Apart from that, rrree-member to behave normally at all times. Is everything clear? Any qvestions?"

"I have one question, Your Grandness," said a voice in the audience. "What happens if one of the chocolates we are giving away in our shops gets eaten by a grown-up?"

"That's just too bad for the grrrown-up," said The Grand High Witch. "This meeting is over!" she shouted. "Out you go!"

The witches stood up and began gathering their things together. I was watching them through the crack and hoping to heaven they would hurry up and leave so that I might be safe at last.

"*Wait!*" shrieked one of the witches in the back row. "*Hold everything!*" Her shrieking voice echoed through the Ballroom like a trumpet. All the witches suddenly stopped and turned and looked towards the speaker. She was one of the taller witches and I could see her standing there with her head tilted back and her nose in the air and she was sucking in great long breaths of air through those curvy pink sea-shelly nostrils of hers.

"*Wait!*" she shouted again.

"What is it?" the others cried out.

"Dogs' droppings!" she yelled. "Just then I got a whiff of dogs' droppings!"

"Surely not!" the others shouted. "There couldn't be!"

"Yes yes!" shouted the first witch. "There it is again! It's not strong! But it's there! I mean it's here! It's definitely somewhere not too far away!"

"Vot's going on down there?" shouted The Grand High Witch, glaring down from the platform.

"Mildred's just got a whiff of dogs' droppings, Your Grandness!" someone called back to her.

"Vot rrrubbish is this?" shouted The Grand High Witch. "She has dogs' drrroppings on the brain! There are no children in this rrroom!"

"Hang on!" cried the witch called Mildred. "Hang on everybody! Don't move! I'm getting it again!" Her huge curvy nose-holes were waving in and out like a pair of fish-tails. "It's getting stronger! It's hitting me harder now! Can't the rest of you smell it?"

All the noses of all the witches in that room went up in the air, and all the nostrils began to suck and sniff.

"She's right!" cried another voice. "She's absolutely right! Dogs' droppings it is, strong and foul!"

In a matter of seconds, the entire assembly of witches had taken up the dreaded cry of dogs' droppings. "Dogs' droppings!" they shouted. "The room is full of it! Poo! Poo-oo-oo-oo-oo-oo-ooo! Why did we not smell it before? It stinks like a sewer! Some little swine must be hiding not so very far away from here!"

"Find it!" screamed The Grand High Witch. "Trrrack it down! Rrrootle it out! Follow your noses till you get it!"

The hairs on my head were standing up like the bristles of a nail-brush and a cold sweat was breaking out all over me.

"Rrrootle it out, this small lump of dung!" screeched The Grand High Witch. "Don't let it escape! If it is in here it has observed the most secret things! It must be exterrrminated immediately!"

Metamorphosis

I remember thinking to myself, *There is no escape for me now! Even if I make a run for it and manage to dodge the lot of them, I still won't get out because the doors are chained and locked! I'm finished! I'm done for! Oh Grandmamma, what are they going to do to me?*

I looked round and I saw a hideous painted and powdered witch's face staring down at me, and the face opened its mouth and yelled triumphantly, "It's here! It's behind the screen! Come and get it!" The witch reached out a gloved hand and grabbed me by the hair but I twisted free and jumped away. I ran, oh how I ran! The sheer terror of it all put wings on my feet! I flew around the outside of the great Ballroom and not one of them had a chance of catching me. As I came level with the doors, I paused and tried to open them but the big chain was on them and they didn't even rattle.

The witches were not bothering to chase me. They simply stood there in small groups, watching me and knowing for certain that there was no way I could escape. Several of them were holding their noses with gloved fingers and there were cries of, "Poo! What a stink! We can't stand this much longer!"

"Catch it then, you idiots!" screamed The

Grand High Witch from up on the platform. "Sprrread out in a line across the room and close in on it and grab it! Corner this filthy little gumboil and seize it and bring it up here to me!"

The witches spread out as they were told. They advanced towards me, some from one end, some from the other, and some came down the middle between the rows of empty chairs. They were bound to get me now. They had me cornered.

From sheer and absolute terror, I began to scream. "*Help!*" I screamed, turning my head towards the doors in the hope that somebody outside might hear me. "Help! Help! Hel-l-l-lp!"

"Get it!" shouted The Grand High Witch. "Grrrab hold of it! Stop it yelling!"

They rushed at me then, and about five of them grabbed me by the arms and legs and lifted me clear off the ground. I went on screaming, but one of them clapped a gloved hand over my mouth and that stopped me.

"Brrring it here!" shouted The Grand High Witch. "Brrring the spying little vurm up here to me!"

I was carried on to the platform with my arms and legs held tight by many hands, and I lay there suspended in the air, facing the ceiling. I saw The Grand High Witch standing over me, grinning at me in the most horrible way. She held up the small blue bottle of Mouse-Maker and she said, "Now for a little medicine! Hold his nose to make him open his mouth!"

Strong fingers pinched my nose. I kept my

117

mouth closed tight and held my breath. But I couldn't do it for long. My chest was bursting. I opened my mouth to get one big quick breath of air and as I did so, The Grand High Witch poured the entire contents of the little bottle down my throat!

Oh, the pain and the fire! It felt as though a kettleful of boiling water had been poured into my mouth. My throat was going up in flames! Then very quickly the frightful burning searing scorching feeling started spreading down into my chest and into my tummy and on and on into my arms and legs and all over my body! I screamed and screamed but once again the gloved hand was clapped over my lips. The next thing I felt was my skin beginning to tighten. How else can I describe it? It was quite literally a tightening and a shrinking of the skin all over my body from the top of my head to the tips of my fingers to the ends of my toes! I felt as though I was a balloon and somebody was twisting the top of the balloon and twisting and twisting and the balloon was getting smaller and smaller and the skin was getting tighter and tighter and soon it was going to burst.

Then the *squeezing* began. This time I was inside a suit of iron and somebody was turning a screw, and with each turn of the screw the iron suit became smaller and smaller so that I was squeezed like an orange into a pulpy mess with the juice running out of my sides.

After that there came a fierce prickling sensation all over my skin (or what was left of my skin) as though tiny needles were forcing their way out through the surface of the skin from the inside, and this, I realise now, was the growing of the mouse-fur.

Far away in the distance, I heard the voice of The Grand High Witch yelling, "Five hundred doses! This stinking little carbuncle has had five hundred doses and the alarm-clock has been smashed and now vee are having *instantaneous action*!" I heard clapping and cheering and I remember thinking: *I am not myself any longer! I have gone clear out of my own skin!*

I noticed that the floor was only an inch from my nose.

I noticed also a pair of little furry front paws resting on the floor. I was able to move those paws. They were mine!

At that moment, I realised that I was not a little boy any longer. I was A MOUSE.

"Now for the mouse-trrrap!" I heard The Grand High Witch yelling. "I've got it right here! And here's a piece of cheese!"

But I wasn't going to wait for *that*. I was off across the platform like a streak of lightning! I was astonished at my own speed! I leapt over witches' feet right and left, and in no time at all I was down the steps and on to the floor of the Ballroom itself and skittering off among the rows of chairs. What I especially liked was the fact that I made no sound at all as I ran. I was a swift and silent mover. And quite amazingly, the pain had all gone now. I was feeling quite remarkably well. *It is not a bad thing after all,* I thought to myself, *to be tiny as well as speedy when there is a bunch of dangerous females after your blood.* I selected the back leg of a chair and squeezed up against it and kept very still.

In the distance, The Grand High Witch was shouting, "Leave the little stinkpot alone! It is not vurth bothering about! It is only a mouse now! Somebody else vill soon catch it! Let us get out of here! The meeting is over! Unlock the doors and shove off to the Sunshine Terrace to have tea vith that idiotic Manager!"

Bruno

I peeped round the leg of the chair and watched the hundreds of witches' feet walking out through the doors of the Ballroom. When they had all gone and the place was absolutely silent, I began to move cautiously about on the floor. Suddenly I remembered Bruno. He must surely be around here somewhere, too. "Bruno!" I called out.

I wasn't seriously expecting that I would be able to speak at all now that I had become a mouse, so I got the shock of my life when I heard my own voice, my own perfectly normal rather loud voice, coming out of my tiny mouth.

It was wonderful. I was thrilled. I tried it again. "Bruno Jenkins, where are you?" I called out. "If you can hear me, give a shout!"

My voice was exactly the same and just as loud as it had been when I was a boy. "Hey there, Bruno Jenkins!" I called. "Where are you?"

There was no answer.

I pottered about between the seat-legs trying to get used to being so close to the ground. I decided I rather liked it. You are probably wondering why I wasn't depressed at all. I found myself thinking, *What's so wonderful about being a little boy anyway? Why is that necessarily any better than being a mouse? I know that mice get hunted and they* sometimes get poisoned or caught in traps. But little boys sometimes get killed, too. Little boys can be run over by motor-cars or they can die of some awful illness. Little boys have to go to school. Mice don't. Mice don't have to pass exams. Mice don't have to worry about money. Mice, as far as I can see, have only two enemies, humans and cats. My grandmother is a human, but I know for certain that she will always love me whoever I am. And she never, thank goodness, keeps a cat. When mice grow up, they don't ever have to go to war and fight against other mice. Mice, I felt pretty certain, all like each other. People don't.

Yes, I told myself, I don't think it is at all a bad thing to be a mouse.

I was wandering around the Ballroom floor thinking about all this when I spotted another mouse. It was crouching on the floor holding a piece of bread in its front paws and nibbling away at it with great gusto.

It had to be Bruno. "Hello, Bruno," I said.

He glanced up at me for about two seconds, then went right on guzzling.

"What have you found?" I asked him.

"One of them dropped it," he answered. "It's a fish-paste sandwich. Pretty good."

He too spoke with a perfectly normal voice. One would have expected that a mouse (if it was going to talk at all) would do so with the smallest and squeakiest voice you could imagine. It was terrifically funny to hear the voice of the rather loud-mouthed Bruno coming out of that tiny mouse's throat.

"Listen, Bruno," I said. "Now that we are both mice, I think we ought to start thinking a bit about the future."

He stopped eating and stared at me with small black eyes. "What do you mean *we?*" he said. "The fact that you're a mouse has nothing to do with me."

"But you're a mouse, too, Bruno."

"Don't be a fool," he said. "I'm not a mouse."

"I'm afraid you are, Bruno."

"I most certainly am not!" he shouted. "Why are you insulting me? I haven't been rude to you! Why do you call *me* a mouse?"

"Don't you know what's happened to you?" I said.

"What on earth are you talking about?" Bruno said.

"I have to inform you", I said, "that not very long ago the witches turned you into a mouse. Then they did it to me."

"You're lying!" he cried. "I'm not a mouse!"

"If you hadn't been so busy guzzling that sandwich," I said, "you would have noticed your hairy paws. Take a look at them."

Bruno looked down at his paws. He jumped. "Good grief!" he cried. "I *am* a mouse! You wait till my father hears about this!"

"He may think it's an improvement," I said.

"I don't want to be a mouse!" Bruno shouted, jumping up and down. "I refuse to be a mouse! I'm Bruno Jenkins!"

"There are worse things than being a mouse," I said. "You can live in a hole."

"I don't want to live in a hole!" Bruno shouted.

"And you can creep into the larder at night," I said, "and nibble through all the packets of raisins and cornflakes and chocolate biscuits and everything else you can find. You can stay there all night eating yourself silly. That's what mice do."

"Now that's a thought," Bruno said, perking up a bit. "But how am I going to open the door of the fridge to get at the cold chicken and all the leftovers? That's something I do every evening at home."

"Maybe your rich father will get you a special little mouse-fridge all to yourself," I said. "One that you can open."

"You say a witch did this to me?" Bruno said. "Which witch?"

"The one who gave you the chocolate bar in the hotel lobby yesterday," I told him. "Don't you remember?"

"The filthy old cow!" he shouted. 'I'll get her for this! Where is she? Who is she?"

"Forget it," I said. "You don't have a hope. Your biggest problem at the moment is your parents. How are they going to take this? Will they treat you with sympathy and kindness?"

Bruno considered this for a moment. "I think", he said, "that my father is going to be a bit put out."

"And your mother?"

"She's terrified of mice," Bruno said.

"Then you've got a problem, haven't you?"

"Why only me?" he said. "What about you?"

"My grandmother will understand perfectly," I said."She knows all about witches."

Bruno took another bite of his sandwich. "What do you suggest?" he said.

"I suggest we both go first of all and consult my grandmother," I said. "She'll know exactly what to do."

I moved towards the doors which were standing open. Bruno, still grasping part of the sandwich in one paw, followed after me.

"When we get out into the corridor," I said,

126

"we're going to run like mad. Stick close to the wall all the way and follow me. Do not talk and do not let anyone see you. Don't forget that just about anyone who catches sight of you will try to kill you."

I snatched the sandwich out of his paw and threw it away. "Here goes," I said. "Keep behind me."

Hello Grandmamma

As soon as I was out of the Ballroom, I took off like a flash. I streaked down the corridor, went through the Lounge and the Reading-Room and the Library and the Drawing-Room and came to the stairs. Up the stairs I went, jumping quite easily from one to the other, keeping well in against the wall all the time. "Are you with me, Bruno?" I whispered.

"Right here," he said.

My grandmother's room and my own were on the fifth floor. It was quite a climb, but we made it without meeting a single person on the way because everyone was using the lift. On the fifth floor, I raced along the corridor to the door of my grandmother's room. A pair of her shoes was standing outside the door to be cleaned. Bruno was alongside me. "What do we do now?" he said.

Suddenly, I caught sight of a chambermaid coming along the corridor towards us. I saw at once that she was the one who had reported me to the manager for keeping white mice. Not, therefore, the sort of person I wanted to meet in my present condition. "Quick!" I said to Bruno. "Hide in one of those shoes!" I hopped into one shoe and Bruno hopped into the other. I waited for the maid to walk past us. She didn't. When she came to the shoes, she bent down and picked them up. In doing this, she put her hand right inside the one I was hiding in. When one of her fingers touched me, I bit it. It was a silly thing to do, but I did it instinctively, without thinking. The maid let out a scream that must have been heard by ships far out in the English Channel, and she dropped the shoes and ran like the wind down the corridor.

My grandmother's door opened. "What on earth is going on out here?" she said. I darted between her legs into her room and Bruno followed me.

"Close the door, Grandmamma!" I cried. "Please hurry!"

She looked around and saw two small brown mice on the carpet. "Please close it," I said, and this time she actually saw me talking and recognised my voice. She froze and became absolutely motionless. Every part of her body, her fingers and hands and arms and head became suddenly as stiff as a marble statue. Her face turned even paler than marble and her eyes were stretched so wide I could see the whites all around them. Then she started to tremble. I thought she was going to faint and fall over.

"Please close the door quickly, Grandmamma," I said. "That awful maid might come in."

She somehow managed to gather herself together enough to close the door. She leaned against it, staring down at me white-faced and shaking all over. I saw tears beginning to come out of her eyes and go dribbling down her cheeks.

"Don't cry, Grandmamma," I said. "Things could be a lot worse. I did get away from them. I'm still alive. So is Bruno."

Very slowly, she bent down and picked me up with one hand. Then she picked Bruno up with the other hand and put us both on the table. There was a bowl of bananas in the centre of the table and Bruno jumped straight into it and began tearing away with his teeth at one of the banana skins to get at the fruit inside.

My grandmother grasped the arm of her chair to steady herself, but her eyes never left me.

"Sit down, dear Grandmamma," I said.

She collapsed into her chair.

"Oh, my darling," she murmured and now the tears were really streaming down her cheeks. "Oh, my poor sweet darling. What *have* they done to you?"

"I know what they've done, Grandmamma, and I know what I am, but the funny thing is that I don't honestly feel especially bad about it. I don't

130

even feel angry. In fact, I feel rather good. I know I'm not a boy any longer and I never will be again, but I'll be quite all right as long as there's always you to look after me." I was not just trying to console her. I was being absolutely honest about the way I felt. You may think it odd that I wasn't weeping myself. It *was* odd. I simply can't explain it.

"Of course I'll look after you," my grandmother murmured. "Who is the other one?"

"That was a boy called Bruno Jenkins," I told her. "They got him first."

My grandmother took a new long black cigar out of a case in her handbag and put it in her mouth. Then she got out a box of matches. She struck a match but her fingers were shaking so much that the flame kept missing the end of the cigar. When she got it lit at last, she took a long pull and sucked in the smoke. That seemed to calm her down a bit.

"Where did it happen?" she whispered. "Where is the witch now? Is she in the hotel?"

"Grandmamma," I said. "It wasn't just one. It was *hundreds*! They're all over the place! They're right here in the hotel this very moment!"

She leant forward and stared at me. "You don't mean . . . you don't actually mean . . . you don't mean to tell me they're holding the Annual Meeting right here in the hotel?"

"They've held it, Grandmamma! It's finished! I heard it all! And all of them including The Grand High Witch herself are downstairs now! They're

131

pretending they're the Royal Society for the Prevention of Cruelty to Children! They're all having tea with the Manager!"

"And they caught you?"

"They smelt me out," I said.

"Dogs' droppings, was it?" she said, sighing.

"I'm afraid so. But it wasn't strong. They very nearly didn't smell me because I hadn't had a bath for ages."

"Children should *never* have baths," my grandmother said. "It's a dangerous habit."

"I agree, Grandmamma."

She paused, sucking at her cigar.

"Do you *really* mean to tell me that they are now all downstairs having tea?" she said.

"I'm certain of it, Grandmamma."

There was another pause. I could see the old glint of excitement slowly coming back into my grandmother's eyes, and all of a sudden she sat up very straight in her chair and said sharply, "Tell me everything, right from the beginning. And please hurry."

I took a deep breath and began to talk. I told about going to the Ballroom and hiding behind the screen to do my mouse-training. I told about the notice saying Royal Society for the Prevention of Cruelty to Children. I told her all about the women coming in and sitting down and about the small woman who appeared on the stage and took off her mask. But when it came to describing what her face looked like underneath the mask, I simply couldn't find the right words. "It was horrible, Grandmamma!" I said. "Oh, it was so horrible! It was ... it was like something that was going rotten!"

"Go on," my grandmother said. "Don't stop."

Then I told her about all the others taking off their wigs and their gloves and their shoes, and how I saw before me a sea of bald pimply heads and how the women's fingers had little claws and how their feet had no toes.

133

My grandmother had come forward now in her armchair so that she was sitting right on the edge of it. Both her hands were cupped over the gold knob of the stick that she always used when walking, and she was staring at me with eyes as bright as two stars.

Then I told her how The Grand High Witch had shot out the fiery white-hot sparks and how they had turned one of the other witches into a puff of smoke.

"I've heard about that!" my grandmother cried out excitedly. "But I never quite believed it! You are the first non-witch ever to see it happening! It is The Grand High Witch's most famous punishment! It is known as 'getting fried', and all the other witches are petrified of having it done to them! I am told that The Grand High Witch makes it a rule to fry at least one witch at each Annual Meeting. She does it in order to keep the rest of them on their toes."

"But they don't *have* any toes, Grandmamma."

"I *know* they don't, my darling, but please go on."

So then I told my grandmother about the Delayed Action Mouse-Maker, and when I came to the bit about turning all the children of England into mice, she actually leapt out of her chair shouting, "I knew it! I knew they were brewing up something tremendous!"

"We've got to stop them," I said.

She turned and stared at me. "You can't stop witches," she said. "Just look at the power that

134

terrible Grand High Witch has in her eyes alone!
She could kill any of us at any time with those
white-hot sparks of hers! You saw it yourself!"

"Even so, Grandmamma, we've still got to stop
her from turning all the children of England into
mice."

"You haven't quite finished," she said. "Tell me
about Bruno. How did they get *him*?"

So I described how Bruno Jenkins had come in
and how I had actually seen him with my own
eyes being shrunk into a mouse. My grandmother
looked at Bruno who was guzzling away in the
bowl of bananas.

"Does he never stop eating?" she asked.

"Never," I said. "Can you explain something to
me, Grandmamma?"

"I'll try," she said. She reached out and lifted me off the table and put me on her lap. Very gently, she began stroking the soft fur along my back. It felt nice. "What is it you want to ask me, my darling?" she said.

"The thing I don't understand", I said, "is how Bruno and I are still able to talk and think just as we did before."

"It's quite simple," my grandmother said. "All they've done is to shrink you and give you four legs and a furry coat, but they haven't been able to change you into a one hundred per cent mouse. You are still yourself in everything except your appearance. You've still got your own mind and your own brain and your own voice, and thank goodness for that."

"So I'm not really an *ordinary* mouse at all," I said. "I'm a sort of mouse-person."

"Quite right," she said. "You are a human in mouse's clothing. You are very special."

We sat there in silence for a few moments while my grandmother went on stroking me very gently with one finger and puffing her cigar with the other hand. The only sound in the room was made by Bruno as he attacked the bananas in the bowl. But I wasn't doing nothing as I lay there on her lap. I was thinking like mad. My brain was whizzing as it had never whizzed before.

"Grandmamma," I said. "I may have a bit of an idea."

"Yes, my darling. What is it?"

"The Grand High Witch told them her room

was number 454. Right?"

"Right," she said.

"Well, *my* room is number 554. Mine, 554, is on the fifth floor, so hers, 454, will be on the fourth floor."

"That is correct," my grandmother said.

"Then don't you think it's possible that room 454 is directly underneath room 554?"

"That's more than likely," she said. "These modern hotels are all built like boxes of bricks. But what if it is?"

"Would you please take me out on to my balcony so I can look down," I said.

All the rooms in the Hotel Magnificent had small private balconies. My grandmother carried me through into my own bedroom and out on to my balcony. We both peered down to the balcony immediately below.

"Now if that *is* her room," I said, "then I'll bet I could climb down there somehow and get in."

"And get caught all over again," my grandmother said. "I won't allow it."

"At this moment," I said, "all the witches are down on the Sunshine Terrace having tea with the Manager. The Grand High Witch probably won't be back until six o'clock or just before. That's when she's going to dish out supplies of that foul formula to the ancient ones who are too old to climb trees after gruntles' eggs."

"And what if you did manage to get into her room?" my grandmother said. "What then?"

"Then I should try to find the place where she

137

keeps her supply of Delayed Action Mouse-Maker, and if I succeeded then I would steal one bottle of it and bring it back here."

"Could you carry it?"

"I think so," I said. "It's a very small bottle."

"I'm frightened of that stuff," my grandmother said. "What would you do with it if you did manage to get it?"

"One bottle is enough for five hundred people," I said. "That would give each and every witch down there a double dose at least. We could turn them all into mice."

My grandmother jumped about an inch in the air. We were out on my balcony and there was a drop of about a million feet below us and I very nearly bounced out of her hand over the railings when she jumped.

"Be careful with me, Grandmamma," I said.

"What an idea!" she cried. "It's fantastic! It's tremendous! You're a genius, my darling!"

"Wouldn't it be something?" I said. "Wouldn't that really be something?"

"We'd get rid of every witch in England in one swoop!" she cried. "*And* The Grand High Witch into the bargain!"

"We've got to try it," I said.

"Listen," she said, nearly dropping me over the balcony once again in her excitement. "If we brought this off, it would be the greatest triumph in the whole history of witchery!"

"There's a lot of work to do," I said.

"Of course there's a lot of work to do," she said.

"Just for a start, supposing you did manage to get hold of one of those bottles, how would you get it into their food?"

"We'll work that out later," I said. "Let's try to get the stuff first. How can we find out for sure if that's her room just below us?"

"We shall check it out immediately!" my grandmother cried. "Come along! There's not a second to waste!" Carrying me in one hand, she went bustling out of the bedroom and along the corridor, banging her stick on the carpet with each step she took. We went down the stairs one flight to the fourth floor. The bedrooms on either side of the corridor had their numbers painted on the doors in gold.

"Here it is!" my grandmother cried. "Number 454." She tried the door. It was locked of course. She looked up and down the long empty hotel corridor. "I do believe you're right," she said. "This room is almost certainly directly below yours." She marched back along the corridor, counting the number of doors from The Grand High Witch's room to the staircase. There were six.

She climbed back up to the fifth floor and repeated the exercise.

"She *is* directly below you!" my grandmother cried out. "Her room is right below yours!"

She carried me back into my own bedroom and went out once again on to the balcony. "That's her balcony down there," she said. "And what's more, the door from her balcony into her bedroom is wide open! How are you going to climb down?"

"I don't know," I said. Our rooms were in the front of the hotel and they looked down on to the beach and the sea. Immediately below my balcony, thousands of feet below, I could see a fence of spiked railings. If I fell, I'd be a gonner.

"I've got it!" my grandmother cried. With me in her hand, she rushed back into her own room and began rummaging in the chest-of-drawers. She came out with a ball of blue knitting-wool. One end of it was attached to some needles and a half-finished sock she had been knitting for me. "This is perfect," she said. "I shall put you in the sock and lower you down on to The Grand High Witch's balcony. But we *must* hurry! Any moment now that monster will be returning to her room!"

140

The Mouse-Burglar

My grandmother hustled me back into my own bedroom and out on to the balcony. "Are you ready?" she asked. "I'm going to put you in the sock now."

"I hope I can manage this," I said. "I'm only a little mouse."

"You'll manage," she said. "Good luck, my darling." She popped me into the sock and started lowering me over the balcony. I crouched inside the sock and held my breath. Through the stitches I could see out quite clearly. Miles below me, the children playing on the beach were the size of beetles. The sock started swinging in the breeze. I looked up and saw my grandmother's head sticking out over the railings of the balcony above. "You're nearly there!" she called out. "Here we go! Gently does it. You're down!"

I felt a slight bump. "In you go!" my grandmother was shouting. "Hurry, hurry, hurry! Search the room!"

I jumped out of the sock and ran into The Grand High Witch's bedroom. There was the same musty smell about the place that I had noticed in the Ballroom. It was the stench of witches. It reminded me of the smell inside the men's public lavatory at our local railway-station.

As far as I could see, the room was tidy enough.
There was no sign anywhere that it was inhabited
by anyone but an ordinary person. But then there
wouldn't be, would there? No witch would be
stupid enough to leave anything suspicious lying

around for the hotel maid to see.

Suddenly I saw a frog jumping across the carpet and disappearing under the bed. I jumped myself.

"*Hurry up!*" came my grandmother's voice from somewhere high up outside. "Grab the stuff and *get out!*"

I started skittering round and trying to search the room. This wasn't so easy. I couldn't, for example, open any of the drawers. I couldn't open the doors of the big wardrobe either. I stopped skittering about. I sat in the middle of the floor and had a think. If The Grand High Witch wanted to hide something top secret, where would she put it? Certainly not in any ordinary drawer. Not in the wardrobe either. It was too obvious. I jumped up on to the bed to get a better view of the room. *Hey*, I thought, *what about under the mattress?* Very carefully, I lowered myself over the edge of the bed and wormed my way underneath the mattress. I had to push forward hard to make any headway, but I kept at it. I couldn't see a thing. I was scrabbling about under the mattress when my head suddenly bumped against something hard *inside* the mattress above me. I reached up and felt it with my paw. Could it be a little bottle? It *was* a little bottle! I could trace the shape of it through the cloth of the mattress. And right alongside it, I felt another hard lump, and another and another. The Grand High Witch must have slit open the mattress and put all the bottles inside and then sewn it all up again. I began tearing away frantically at the mattress cloth above my head with my teeth. My front teeth were extremely sharp and it didn't take me long to make a small hole. I climbed into the hole and grabbed a bottle by the neck. I pushed it down through the hole in the mattress and climbed out after it.

Walking backwards and dragging the bottle behind me, I managed to reach the edge of the mattress. I rolled the bottle off the bed on to the carpet. It bounced but it didn't break. I jumped down off the bed. I examined the little bottle. It was identical to the one The Grand High Witch had had in the Ballroom. There was a label on this one. FORMULA 86, it said. DELAYED ACTION MOUSE-MAKER. Then it said, *This bottle contains five hundred doses*. Eureka! I felt tremendously pleased with myself.

Three frogs came hopping out from under the bed. They crouched on the carpet, staring at me with large black eyes. I stared back at them. Those huge eyes were the saddest things I had ever seen. It suddenly occurred to me that almost certainly once upon a time they had been children, those frogs, before The Grand High Witch had got hold of them. I stood there clutching the bottle and staring at the frogs. "Who are you?" I asked them.

At that exact moment, I heard a key turning in the lock of the door and the door burst open and The Grand High Witch swept into the room. The frogs jumped underneath the bed again in one quick hop. I darted after them, still clutching the bottle, and I ran back against the wall and squeezed in behind one of the bedposts. I heard feet walking on the carpet. I peeped round the bedpost. The three frogs were clustered together under the middle of the bed. Frogs cannot hide like mice. They cannot run like mice, either. All they can do, poor things, is to hop about rather clumsily.

Suddenly The Grand High Witch's face came into view, peering under the bed. I popped my head back behind the bedpost. "So there you are, my little frrroggies," I heard her saying. "You can stay vhere you are until I go to bed tonight, then I shall

thrrrow you out of the vindow and the seagulls can
have you for supper."

Suddenly very loud and clear there came the
sound of my grandmother's voice through the open
balcony door. "Hurry up, my darling!" it shouted.
"Do hurry up! You'd better come out quickly!"

"Who is calling?" snapped The Grand High
Witch. I peeped round the bedpost again and saw
her walking across the carpet to the balcony door.
"Who is this on my balcony?" she muttered.
"Who is it? Who dares to trrrespass on my balcony?" She went through the door on to the balcony itself.

"Vot is this knitting-vool hanging down here?" I heard her saying.

"Oh, hello," came my grandmother's voice. "I just dropped my knitting over the balcony by mistake. But it's all right. I've got hold of one end of it. I can pull it up by myself, thank you all the same." I marvelled at the coolness of her voice.

"Who vur you talking to just now?" snapped The Grand High Witch. "Who vur you telling to hurry up and come out qvickly?"

"I was talking to my little grandson," I heard my grandmother saying. "He's been in the bathroom for hours and it's time he came out. He sits in there reading books and he forgets completely where he is! Do *you* have any children, my dear?"

"I do not!" shouted The Grand High Witch, and she came quickly back into the bedroom, *slamming the balcony door behind her*.

I was cooked. My escape route was closed. I was shut up in the room with The Grand High Witch and three terrified frogs. I was just as terrified as the frogs. I was quite sure that if I was spotted, I would be caught and thrown out over the balcony for the seagulls.

There came a knock on the bedroom door. "Vot is it this time?" shouted The Grand High Witch.

"It is we ancient ones," said a meek voice from behind the door. "It is six o'clock and we have come to collect the bottles that you promised us, O Your Grandness."

I saw her crossing the carpet towards the door.

147

The door was opened and then I saw a whole lot of
feet and shoes beginning to enter the room. They
were coming in slowly and hesitantly, as though
the owners of those shoes were frightened of enter-
ing. "Come in! Come in!" snapped The Grand
High Witch. "Do not stand out there dithering in
the corrri-dor! I don't have all night!"

I saw my chance. I jumped out from behind the
bedpost and ran like lightning towards the open

door. I jumped over several pairs of shoes on the way and in three seconds I was out in the corridor, still clutching the precious bottle to my chest. No one had seen me. There were no shouts of *Mouse! Mouse!* All I could hear were the voices of the ancient witches burbling their silly sentences about "How kind Your Grandness is" and all the rest of it. I went scampering down the corridor to the stairs and up one flight. I went to the fifth floor and then along the corridor again until I came to the door of my own bedroom. Thank goodness there was no one in sight. Using the bottom of the little bottle, I began tap-tap-tapping on the door. *Tap tap tap tap,* I went. *Tap tap tap . . . tap tap tap . . .* Would my grandmother hear me? I thought that she must. The bottle made quite a loud tap each time it struck. *Tap tap tap . . . tap tap tap . . .* Just so long as nobody came along the corridor.

But the door didn't open. I decided to take a risk. "Grandmamma!" I shouted as loudly as I possibly could. "Grandmamma! It's me! Let me in!"

I heard her feet coming across the carpet and the door opened. I went in like an arrow. "I've done it!" I cried, jumping up and down. "I've got it, Grandmamma! Look, here it is! I've got a whole bottle of it!"

She closed the door. She bent down and picked me up and hugged me. "Oh my darling!" she cried. "Thank heavens you're safe!" She took the little bottle from me and read the label aloud. " 'Formula 86 Delayed Action Mouse-Maker!' " she read. " 'This bottle contains five hundred doses!'

You brilliant darling boy! You're a wonder! You're a marvel! How on earth did you get out of her room?"

"I nipped out when the ancient witches were coming in," I told her. "It was all a bit hairy, Grandmamma. I wouldn't want to do it again."

"I saw her too!" my grandmother said.

"I know you did, Grandmamma. I heard you talking to each other. Didn't you think she was absolutely foul?"

"She's a murderer," my grandmother said. "She's the most evil woman in the entire world!"

"Did you see her mask?" I asked.

"It's amazing," my grandmother said. "It looks just like a real face. Even though I knew it was a mask, I still couldn't tell. Oh, my darling!" she cried, giving me a hug. "I thought I'd never see you again! I'm so happy you got away!"

Mr and Mrs Jenkins Meet Bruno

My grandmother carried me back into her own bedroom and put me on the table. She set the precious bottle down beside me. "What time are those witches having supper in the Dining-Room?" she asked.

"Eight o'clock," I said.

She looked at her watch. "It is now ten-past six," she said. "We've got until eight o'clock to work out our next move." Suddenly, her eye fell upon Bruno. He was still in the banana bowl on the table. He had eaten three bananas and was now attacking a fourth. He had become immensely fat.

"That's quite enough," my grandmother said, lifting him out of the bowl and putting him on the table-top. "I think it's time we returned this little fellow to the bosom of his family. Don't you agree, Bruno?"

Bruno scowled at her. I had never seen a mouse scowl before, but he managed it. "My parents let me eat as much as I want," he said. "I'd rather be with them than with you."

"Of course you would," my grandmother said. "Do you know where your parents might be at this moment?"

"They were in the Lounge not long ago," I said. "I saw them sitting there as we dashed through on our way up here."

"Right," my grandmother said. "Let's go and see if they are still there. Do you want to come along?" she added, looking at me.

"Yes, please," I said.

"I shall put you both in my handbag," she said. "Keep quiet and stay out of sight. If you must peep out now and again, don't show more than your nose."

Her handbag was a large bulgy black-leather affair with a tortoise-shell clasp. She picked up Bruno and me and popped us into it. "I shall leave the clasp undone," she said. "But be sure to keep out of sight."

I had no intention of keeping out of sight. I wanted to see everything. I seated myself in a little side-pocket inside the bag, near the clasp, and from there I was able to poke my head out whenever I wanted to.

"Hey!" Bruno called out. "Give me the rest of that banana I was eating."

"Oh all right," my grandmother said. "Anything to keep you quiet." She dropped the half-eaten

152

banana into the bag, then slung the bag over her arm and marched out of the room and went thumping along the corridor with her walking-stick.

We went down in the lift to the ground floor and made our way through the Reading-Room to the Lounge. And there, sure enough, sat Mr and Mrs Jenkins in a couple of armchairs with a low round glass-covered table between them. There were several other groups in there as well, but the Jenkinses were the only couple sitting alone. Mr Jenkins was reading a newspaper. Mrs Jenkins was knitting something large and mustard-coloured. Only my nose and eyes were above the clasp of my grandmother's handbag, but I had a super view. I could see everything.

My grandmother, dressed in black lace, went thumping across the floor of the Lounge and halted in front of the Jenkins's table. "Are you Mr and Mrs Jenkins?" she asked.

Mr Jenkins looked at her over the top of his newspaper and frowned. "Yes," he said. "I am Mr Jenkins. What can I do for you, madam?"

"I'm afraid I have some rather alarming news for you," she said. "It's about your son, Bruno."

"What about Bruno?" Mr Jenkins said.

Mrs Jenkins looked up but went on knitting. "What's the little blighter been up to now?" Mr Jenkins asked. "Raiding the kitchen, I suppose."

"It's a bit worse than that," my grandmother said. "Do you think we might go somewhere more private while I tell you about it?"

"Private?" Mr Jenkins said. "Why do we have to be private?"

"This is not an easy thing for me to explain," my grandmother said. "I'd much rather we all went up to your room and sat down before I tell you any more."

Mr Jenkins lowered his paper. Mrs Jenkins stopped knitting. "I don't *want* to go up to my room, madam," Mr Jenkins said. "I'm quite comfortable here, thank you very much." He was a large coarse man and he wasn't used to being pushed around by anybody. "Kindly state your business and then leave us alone," he added. He spoke as though he was addressing someone who was trying to sell him a vacuum-cleaner at the back door.

My poor grandmother, who had been doing her best to be as kind to them as possible, now began to bristle a bit herself. "We really can't talk in here," she said. "There are too many people. This is a rather delicate and personal matter."

"I'll talk where I dashed well want to, madam," Mr Jenkins said. "Come on now, out with it! If Bruno has broken a window or smashed your spectacles, then I'll pay for the damage, but I'm not budging out of this seat!"

One or two other groups in the room were beginning to stare at us now.

"Where *is* Bruno anyway?" Mr Jenkins said. "Tell him to come here and see me."

"He's here already," my grandmother said. "He's in my handbag." She patted the big floppy leather bag with her walking-stick.

"What the heck d'you mean he's in your handbag?" Mr Jenkins shouted.

"Are you trying to be funny?" Mrs Jenkins said, very prim.

"There's nothing funny about this," my grandmother said. "Your son has suffered a rather unfortunate mishap."

"He's always suffering mishaps," Mr Jenkins said. "He suffers from overeating and then he

155

suffers from wind. You should hear him after supper. He sounds like a brass band! But a good dose of castor-oil soon puts him right again. Where *is* the little beggar?"

"I've already told you," my grandmother said. "He's in my handbag. But I do think it might be better if we went somewhere private before you meet him in his present state."

"This woman's mad," Mrs Jenkins said. "Tell her to go away."

"The plain fact is", my grandmother said, "that your son Bruno has been rather drastically altered."

"*Altered!*" shouted Mr Jenkins. "What the devil d'you mean *altered*?"

"Go away!" Mrs Jenkins said. "You're a silly old woman!"

"I am trying to tell you as gently as I possibly can that Bruno really is in my handbag," my grandmother said. "My own grandson actually saw them doing it to him."

"Saw *who* doing *what* to him, for heaven's sake?" shouted Mr Jenkins. He had a black moustache which jumped up and down when he shouted.

"Saw the witches turning him into a mouse," my grandmother said.

"Call the Manager, dear," Mrs Jenkins said to her husband. "Have this mad woman thrown out of the hotel."

At this point, my grandmother's patience came to an end. She fished around in her handbag and

156

found Bruno. She lifted him out and dumped him on the glass-topped table. Mrs Jenkins took one look at the fat little brown mouse who was still chewing a bit of banana and she let out a shriek that rattled the crystals on the chandelier. She sprang out of her chair yelling, "It's a mouse! Take it away! I can't stand the things!"

"It's Bruno," my grandmother said.

"You nasty cheeky old woman!" shouted Mr Jenkins. He started flapping his newspaper at Bruno, trying to sweep him off the table. My grandmother rushed forward and managed to grab hold of him before he was swept away. Mrs Jenkins was still screaming her head off and Mr Jenkins was towering over us and shouting, "Get out of here! How dare you frighten my wife like that! Take your filthy mouse away this instant!"

"Help!" screamed Mrs Jenkins. Her face had gone the colour of the underside of a fish.

"Well, I did my best," my grandmother said, and with that she turned and sailed out of the room, carrying Bruno with her.

The Plan

When we got back to the bedroom, my grand-mother took both me and Bruno out of her hand-bag and put us on the table. "Why on earth didn't you speak up and tell your father who you were?" she said to Bruno.

"Because I had my mouth full," Bruno said. He jumped straight back into the bowl of bananas and went on with his eating.

"What a very disagreeable little boy you are," my grandmother said to him.

"Not boy," I said. "Mouse."

"Quite right, my darling. But we don't have time to worry about him at this moment. We have plans to make. In about an hour and a half's time, all the witches will be going down to supper in the Dining-Room. Right?"

"Right," I said.

"And every one of them has got to be given a dose of Mouse-Maker," she said. "How on earth are we going to do that?"

"Grandmamma," I said. "I think you are forget-ting that a mouse can go places where human beings can't."

"That's quite right," she said. "But even a mouse can't go creeping around on the table-top carrying a bottle and sprinkling Mouse-Maker all over the witches' roast beef without being spotted."

"I wasn't thinking of doing it in the Dining-Room," I said.

"Then where?" she asked.

"In the kitchen," I said, "while their food is being got ready."

My grandmother stared at me. "My darling child," she said slowly, "I do believe that turning you into a mouse has doubled your brain-power!"

"A little mouse", I said, "can go scuttling round the kitchen among the pots and pans, and if he's very careful no one will ever see him."

"Brilliant!" my grandmother cried out. "By golly, I think you've got it!"

"The only thing is," I said, "how will I know which food is theirs? I don't want to put it in the wrong saucepan. It would be disastrous if I turned all the other guests into mice by mistake, and especially you, Grandmamma."

"Then you'll just have to creep into the kitchen and find a good hiding-place and wait . . . and listen. Just lie there in some dark cranny listening and listening to what the cooks are saying . . . and then, with a bit of luck, somebody's going to give you a clue. Whenever they have a very big party to cook for, the food is always prepared separately."

"Right," I said. "That's what I'll have to do. I shall wait there and I shall listen and I shall hope for a bit of luck."

"It's going to be very dangerous," my grandmother said. "Nobody welcomes a mouse in the

159

kitchen. If they see you, they'll squash you to death."

"I won't let them see me," I said.

"Don't forget you'll be carrying the bottle," she said, "so you won't be nearly so quick and nippy."

"I can run quite fast standing up with the bottle in my arms," I said. "I did it just now, don't you remember? I came all the way up from The Grand High Witch's room carrying it."

"What about unscrewing the top?" she said. "That might be difficult for you."

"Let me try," I said. I took hold of the little bottle and using both my front paws, I found I was able to unscrew the cap quite easily.

"That's great," my grandmother said. "You really are a very clever mouse." She glanced at her watch. "At half-past seven," she said, "I shall go down to the Dining-Room for supper with you in my handbag. I shall then release you under the table together with the precious bottle and from then on you'll be on your own. You will have to work your way unseen across the Dining-Room to the door that leads into the kitchen. There will be waiters going in and out of that door all the time. You will have to choose the right moment and nip in behind one of them, but for heaven's sake be sure that you don't get trodden on or squeezed in the door."

"I'll try not to," I said.

"And whatever happens, you mustn't let them catch you."

"Don't go on about it, Grandmamma. You're making me nervous."

"You're a brave little fellow," she said. "I do love you."

"What shall we do with Bruno?" I asked her.

Bruno looked up. "I'm coming with you," he said, speaking with his mouth full of banana. "I'm not going to miss my supper!"

My grandmother considered this for a moment. "I'll take you along," she said, "if you promise to stay in my bag and keep absolutely silent."

"Will you pass food down to me from the table?" Bruno asked.

"Yes," she said, "if you promise to behave yourself. Would *you* like something to eat, my darling?" she said to me.

"No, thank you," I said. "I'm too excited to eat. And I've got to keep fit and frisky for the big job ahead."

"It's a big job all right," my grandmother said. "You'll never do a bigger one."

In the Kitchen

"The time has come!" my grandmother said. "The great moment has arrived! Are you ready, my darling?"

It was exactly half-past seven. Bruno was in the bowl finishing that fourth banana. "Hang on," he said. "Just a few more bites."

"No!" my grandmother said. "We've got to go!" She picked him up and held him tight in her hand. She was very tense and nervous. I had never seen her like that before. "I'm going to put you both in my handbag now," she said, "but I shall leave the clasp undone." She popped Bruno into it first. I waited, clutching the little bottle to my chest. "Now *you*," she said. She picked me up and gave me a kiss on the nose. "Good luck, my darling. Oh, by the way, you do realise you've got a tail, don't you?"

"A what?" I said.

"A tail. A long curly tail."

"I must say that never occurred to me," I said. "Good gracious me, so I have! I can see it now! I can actually move it! It *is* rather grand, isn't it?"

"I mention it only because it might come in useful when you're climbing about in the kitchen," my grandmother said. "You can curl it around and you can hook it on to things and you can swing

162

from it and lower yourself to the ground from high places."

"I wish I'd known this before," I said. "I could have practised using it."

"Too late now," my grandmother said. "We've got to go." She popped me into her handbag with Bruno, and at once I took up my usual perch in the small side-pocket so that I could poke my head out and see what was going on.

My grandmother picked up her walking-stick and out she went into the corridor to the lift. She pressed the button and the lift came up and she got in. There was no one in there with us.

"Listen," she said. "I won't be able to talk to you much once we're in the Dining-Room. If I do, people will think I'm dotty and talking to myself."

The lift reached the ground floor and stopped with a jerk. My grandmother walked out of it and crossed the lobby of the hotel and entered the Dining-Room. It was a huge room with gold decorations on the ceiling and big mirrors around the walls. The regular guests always had their tables reserved for them and most of them were already in their places and starting to eat their suppers. Waiters were buzzing about all over the place, carrying plates and dishes. Our table was a small one beside the right-hand wall about halfway down the room. My grandmother made her way to it and sat down.

Peeping out of the handbag, I could see in the very centre of the room two long tables that were not yet occupied. Each of them carried a notice fixed on to a sort of silver stick and the notices said, RESERVED FOR MEMBERS OF THE RSPCC.

My grandmother looked towards the long tables but said nothing. She unfolded her napkin and spread it over the handbag on her lap. Her hand slid under the napkin and took hold of me gently. With the napkin covering me, she lifted me up close to her face and whispered, "I am about to put you on the floor under the table. The table-cloth reaches almost to the ground so no one will see you. Have you got hold of the bottle?"

"Yes," I whispered back. "I'm ready, Grand-mamma."

Just then, a waiter in a black suit came and stood by our table. I could see his legs from under the napkin and as soon as I heard his voice, I knew who he was. His name was William. "Good evening, madam," he said to my grandmother. "Where is the little gentleman tonight?"

"He's not feeling very well," my grandmother said. "He's staying in his room."

"I'm sorry to hear that," William said. "Today there is green-pea soup to start with, and for the main course you have a choice of either grilled fillet of sole or roast lamb."

"Pea soup and lamb for me, please," my grandmother said. "But don't hurry it, William. I'm in no rush tonight. In fact, you can bring me a glass of dry sherry first."

"Of course, madam," William said, and he went away.

My grandmother pretended she had dropped

something, and as she bent down, she slid me out from under the napkin on to the floor under the table. "Go, darling, go!" she whispered, then she straightened up again.

I was on my own now. I stood clasping the little bottle. I knew exactly where the door into the kitchen was. I had to go about halfway round the enormous Dining-Room to reach it. Here goes, I thought, and like a flash I skittled out from under the table and made for the wall. I had no intention of going across the Dining-Room floor. It was far too risky. My plan was to cling close to the skirting of the wall all the way round until I reached the kitchen door.

I ran. Oh, how I ran. I don't think anyone saw me. They were all too busy eating. But to reach the door leading to the kitchen I had to cross the main entrance to the Dining-Room. I was just about to do this when in poured a great flood of females. I pressed myself against the wall clutching the bottle. At first I saw only the shoes and ankles of these women who were surging in through the door, but when I glanced up a bit higher I knew at once who they were. They were the witches coming in to dinner!

I waited until they had all passed me by, then I dashed on towards the kitchen door. A waiter opened it to go in. I nipped in after him and hid behind a big garbage-bin on the floor. I stayed there for several minutes, just listening to all the talk and the racket. By golly, what a place that kitchen was! The noise! And the steam! And the clatter of pots and pans! And the cooks all shouting! And the waiters all rushing in and out from the Dining-Room yelling the food orders to the cooks! "Four soups and two lambs and two fish for table twenty-eight! Three apple-pies and two strawberry ice-creams for number seventeen!" Stuff like that going on all the time.

Not far above my head there was a handle sticking out from the side of the garbage-bin. Still clutching the bottle, I gave a leap, turned a somersault in the air, and caught hold of the handle with the end of my tail. Suddenly there I was swinging to and fro upside down. It was terrific. I loved it. *This*, I told myself, *is how a trapeze artist in a*

circus must feel as he goes swishing through the air high up in the circus tent. The only difference was that his trapeze could only swing backwards and forwards. My trapeze (my tail) could swing me in any direction I wanted. Perhaps I would become a circus mouse after all.

Just then, a waiter came in with a plate in his hand and I heard him saying, "The old hag on table fourteen says this meat is too tough! She wants another portion!" One of the cooks said, "Gimme her plate!" I dropped to the floor and peeped round the garbage-bin. I saw the cook scrape the meat off the plate and slap another bit on. Then he said, "Come on boys, give her some gravy!" He carried the plate round to everyone in the kitchen and do you know what they did? Every one of those cooks and kitchen-boys spat on to the old lady's plate! "See how she likes it now!" said the cook, handing the plate back to the waiter.

Quite soon another waiter came in and he shouted, "Everyone in the big RSPCC party wants the soup!" That's when I started sitting up and taking notice. I was all ears now. I edged a bit farther round the garbage-bin so that I could see everything that was going on in the kitchen. A man with a tall white hat who must have been the head chef shouted, "Put the soup for the big party in the larger silver soup-tureen!"

I saw the head chef place a huge silver basin on to the wooden side-bench that ran along the whole length of the kitchen against the opposite wall. *Into that silver basin is where the soup is going,* I told myself. *So that's where the stuff in my little bottle must go as well.*

I noticed that high up near the ceiling, above the side-bench, there was a long shelf crammed with saucepans and frying-pans. *If I can somehow clamber up on to that shelf,* I thought, *then I've got it made. I shall be directly above the silver basin.*

But first I must somehow get across to the other side of the kitchen and then up on to the middle shelf. A great idea came to me! Once again, I jumped up and hooked my tail around the handle of the garbage-bin. Then, hanging upside down, I began to swing. Higher and higher

I swung. I was remembering the trapeze artist in the circus I had seen last Easter and the way he had got the trapeze swinging higher and higher and higher and had then let go and gone flying through the air. So just at the right moment, at the top of my swing, I let go with my tail and went soaring clear across the kitchen and made a perfect landing on the middle shelf!

By golly, I thought, what marvellous things a mouse can do! And I'm only a beginner!

No one had seen me. They were all far too busy with their pots and pans. From the middle shelf I somehow managed to shinny up a little water-pipe in the corner, and in no time at all I was up on the very top shelf just under the ceiling, among all the saucepans and the frying-pans. I knew that no one could possibly see me up there. It was a super position, and I began working my way along the shelf until I was directly above the big empty silver basin they were going to pour the soup into. I put down my bottle. I unscrewed the top and crept to the edge of the shelf and quickly poured what was

in it straight into the silver basin below. The next moment, one of the cooks came along with a gigantic saucepan of steaming green soup and poured the whole lot into the silver basin. He put the lid on the basin and shouted, "Soup for the big party all ready to go out!" Then a waiter arrived and carried the silver basin away.

I had done it! Even if I never got back alive to my grandmother, the witches were still going to get the Mouse-Maker! I left the empty bottle behind a large saucepan and began working my way back along the top shelf. It was much easier to move about without the bottle. I began using my tail more and more. I swung from the handle of one saucepan to the handle of another all the way along that top shelf, while far below me cooks and waiters were all bustling about and kettles were steaming and pans were spluttering and pots were boiling and I thought to myself, *Oh boy, this is the*

life! What fun it is to be a mouse doing an exciting job like this! I kept right on swinging. I swung most marvellously from handle to handle, and I

was enjoying myself so much that I completely forgot I was in full view of anyone in the kitchen who might happen to glance upwards. What came next happened so quickly I had no time to save myself. I heard a man's voice yelling, "A mouse! Look at that dirty little mouse!" And I caught a glimpse below me of a white-coated figure in a tall white hat and then there was a flash of steel as the carving-knife whizzed through the air and there was a shoot of pain in the end of my tail and suddenly I was falling and falling head-first towards the floor.

Even as I fell, I knew just what had happened. I knew that the tip of my tail had been cut off and that I was about to crash on to the floor and everyone in the kitchen would be after me. "A mouse!" they were shouting. "A mouse! A mouse! Catch it quick!" I hit the floor and jumped up and ran for my life. All around me there were big black boots going *stamp stamp stamp* and I dodged around them and ran and ran and ran, twisting and turning, and dodging and swerving across the kitchen floor. "Get it!" they were shouting. "Kill it! Stamp on it!" The whole floor seemed to be full of black boots stamping away at me and I dodged and swerved and twisted and turned and then in sheer desperation, hardly knowing what I was doing, wanting only a place to hide, I ran up the trouser-leg of one of the cooks and clung to his sock!

"Hey!" the cook shouted. "Jeepers creepers! He's gone up my trouser! Hold on, boys! I'll get him this time!"

The man's hands began slap-slapping at the trouser-leg and now I really *was* going to get smashed if I didn't move quickly. There was only one way to go and that was up. I dug my little claws into the hairy skin of the man's leg and scuttled upwards, higher and higher, past the calf and past the knee and on to the thigh.

"Holy smoke!" the man was yelling. "It's going all the way up! It's going right up my leg!" I heard shrieks of laughter coming from the other cooks but I can promise you I wasn't laughing myself. I was running for my life. The man's hands were slap-slap-slapping all around me and he was jumping up and down as though he was standing on hot bricks, and I kept climbing and I kept dodging and very soon I reached the very top of the trouser-leg and there was nowhere else to go.

"Help! Help! Help!" the man was screaming. "It's in my knickers! It's running round in my flaming knickers! Get it out! Someone help me to get it out!"

"Take off your trousers, you silly slob!" someone else shouted. "Pull down your pants and we'll soon catch him!"

I was in the middle of the man's trousers now, in the place where the two trouser-legs meet and the zip begins. It was dark and awfully hot in there. I knew I had to keep going. I dashed onward and found the top of the other trouser-leg. I went down it like greased lightning and came out at the bottom of it and once again I was on the floor. I heard the stupid cook still shouting, "It's in my trousers! Get it out! Will somebody *please* help me to get it out before it bites me!" I caught a flashing glimpse of the entire kitchen staff crowding round him and laughing their heads off and nobody saw the little brown mouse as it flew across the floor and dived into a sack of potatoes.

I burrowed down in among the dirty potatoes and held my breath.

The cook must have started taking his trousers right off because now they were shouting, "It's not in there! There's no mice in there, you silly twerp!"

"There was! I swear there was!" the man was shouting back. "You've never *had* a mouse in your trousers! You don't know what it feels like!"

The fact that a tiny little creature like me had caused such a commotion among a bunch of grown-up men gave me a happy feeling. I couldn't help smiling in spite of the pain in my tail.

I stayed where I was until I was sure they had forgotten about me. Then I crept out of the potatoes and cautiously poked my tiny head over the edge of the sack. Once again the kitchen was all of a bustle with cooks and waiters rushing about everywhere. I saw the waiter who had come in earlier with the complaint about tough meat coming in again. "Hey boys!" he shouted. "I asked the old hag if the new bit of meat was any better and she said it was perfectly delicious! She said it was really tasty!"

I had to get out of that kitchen and back to my grandmother. There was only one way to do this. I must make a dash clear across the floor and out through the door behind one of the waiters. I stayed quite still, watching for my chance. My tail was hurting terribly. I curled it round so as to have a look at it. About two inches of it were missing and it was bleeding quite a lot. There was a waiter loading up with a batch of plates full of pink ice-cream. He had a plate in each hand and two more balanced on each arm. He went towards the door. He pushed it open with his shoulder. I leapt out of the sack of potatoes and went across that kitchen floor and into the Dining-Room like a streak of light, and I didn't stop running until I was underneath my grandmother's table.

It was lovely to see my grandmother's feet again in those old-fashioned black shoes with their straps and buttons. I shinnied up one of her legs and landed on her lap. "Hello, Grandmamma!" I whispered. "I'm back! I did it! I poured it all into their soup!"

Her hand came down and caressed me. "Well *done*, my darling!" she whispered back. "Well done you! They are at this very moment eating that soup!" Suddenly, she withdrew her hand. "You're bleeding!" she whispered. "My darling, what's happened to you?"

179

"One of the cooks cut off my tail with a carving-knife," I whispered back. "It hurts like billy-o."

"Let me look at it," she said. She bent her head and examined my tail. "You poor little thing," she whispered. "I'm going to bandage it up with my handkerchief. That will stop the bleeding."

She fished a small lace-edged handkerchief out of her bag and this she somehow managed to wrap around the end of my tail. "You'll be all right

now," she said. "Just try to forget about it. Did you really manage to pour the whole bottle into their soup?"

"Every drop," I said. "Do you think you could put me where I can watch them?"

"Yes," she answered. "My handbag is on your own empty chair beside me. I'm going to pop you in there now and you can peep out as long as you are careful not to be seen. Bruno is there as well, but take no notice of him. I gave him a roll to eat and that's keeping him busy for a while."

Her hand closed around me and I was lifted off

her lap and transferred to the handbag. "Hello, Bruno," I said.

"This is a great roll," he said, nibbling away in the bottom of the bag. "But I wish there was butter on it."

I peered over the top of the handbag. I could see the witches quite clearly sitting at their two long tables in the centre of the room. They had finished their soup now, and the waiters were clearing away the plates. My grandmother had lit up one of her disgusting black cigars and was puffing smoke over everything. All around us the summer-holiday guests in this rather grand hotel were babbling away and tucking into their suppers. About half of them were old people with walking-sticks, but there were also plenty of families with a husband, a wife and several children. They were all well-to-do people. You had to be if you wanted to stay in the Hotel Magnificent.

"That's her, Grandmamma!" I whispered. "That's The Grand High Witch!"

"I know!" my grandmother whispered back. "She's the tiny one in black sitting at the head of the nearest table!"

"She could kill you!" I whispered. "She could kill anyone in this room with her white-hot sparks!"

"Look out!" my grandmother whispered. "The waiter's coming!"

I popped down out of sight and I heard William saying, "Your roast lamb, madam. And which vegetable would you like? Peas or carrots?"

"Carrots, please," my grandmother said. "But no potatoes."

I heard the carrots being dished out. There was a pause. Then my grandmother's voice was whispering, "It's all right. He's gone." I popped my head up again. "Surely no one will notice my little head sticking out like this?" I whispered.

"No," she answered. "I don't suppose they will. *My* problem is I've got to talk to you without moving my lips."

"You're doing beautifully," I said.

"I've counted the witches," she said. "There aren't nearly as many as you thought. You were just guessing, weren't you, when you said two hundred?"

"It just *seemed* like two hundred," I said.

"I was wrong, too," my grandmother said. "I thought there were a lot more witches than this in England."

"How many are there?" I asked.

"Eighty-four," she said.

"There *were* eighty-five," I said. "But one of them got fried."

At that moment, I caught sight of Mr Jenkins, Bruno's father, heading straight for our table. "Look out, Grandmamma!" I whispered. "Here comes Bruno's father!"

Mr Jenkins and His Son

Mr Jenkins came striding up to our table with a very purposeful look on his face.

"Where is that grandson of yours?" he said to my grandmother. He spoke rudely and looked very angry.

My grandmother put on her frostiest look, but didn't answer him.

"My guess is that he and my son Bruno are up to some devilment," Mr Jenkins went on. "Bruno hasn't turned up for his supper and it takes a lot to make that boy miss his food!"

"I must admit he has a very healthy appetite," my grandmother said.

"My feeling is that *you're* in on this as well," Mr Jenkins said. "I don't know who the devil you are and I don't much care, but you played a nasty trick on me and my wife this afternoon. You put a dirty little mouse on the table. That makes me think all three of you are up to something. So if you know where Bruno's hiding, kindly tell me at once."

"That was no trick I played on you," my grandmother said. "That mouse I tried to give you was your own little boy, Bruno. I was being kind to you. I was trying to restore him to the bosom of his family. You refused to take him in."

"What the blazes do you mean, madam?" shouted Mr Jenkins. "My son isn't a *mouse*!" His

183

black moustache was jumping up and down like crazy as he spoke. "Come on, woman! Where is he? Out with it!"

The family at the table nearest to us had all stopped eating and were staring at Mr Jenkins. My grandmother sat there puffing away calmly at her black cigar. "I can well understand your anger, Mr Jenkins," she said. "Any other English father would be just as cross as you are. But over in Norway where I come from, we are quite used to these sort of happenings. We have learnt to accept them as part of everyday life."

"You must be mad, woman!" cried Mr Jenkins. "Where is Bruno? If you don't tell me at once I shall summon the police!"

"Bruno is a mouse," my grandmother said, calm as ever.

"He most certainly is *not* a mouse!" shouted Mr Jenkins.

"Oh yes I am!" Bruno said, poking his head up out of the handbag.

Mr Jenkins leapt about three feet into the air.

"Hello, Dad," Bruno said. He had a silly sort of mousy grin on his face.

Mr Jenkins's mouth dropped open so wide I could see the gold fillings in his back teeth.

"Don't worry, Dad," Bruno went on. "It's not as bad as all that. Just so long as the cat doesn't get me."

"B-B-Bruno!" stammered Mr Jenkins.

"No more school!" said Bruno, grinning a broad and asinine mouse-grin. "No more homework! I

184

shall live in the kitchen cupboard and feast on raisins and honey!"

"B-b-but B-B-Bruno!" stammered Mr Jenkins again. "H-how did this happen?" The poor man had no wind left in his sails at all.

"Witches," my grandmother said. "The witches did it."

"I can't have a mouse for a son!" shrieked Mr Jenkins.

"You've got one," my grandmother said. "Be nice to him, Mr Jenkins."

"Mrs Jenkins will go crazy!" yelled Mr Jenkins. "She can't stand the things!"

"She'll just have to get used to him," my grandmother said. "I hope you don't keep a cat in the house."

"We do! We do!" cried Mr Jenkins. "Topsy is my wife's favourite creature!"

"Then you'll just have to get rid of Topsy," my grandmother said. "Your son is more important than your cat."

"He certainly is!" Bruno shouted from inside the handbag. "You tell Mum she's got to get rid of Topsy before I go home!"

By now half the Dining-Room was watching our little group. Knives and forks and spoons had been put down and all over the place heads were turning round to stare at Mr Jenkins as he stood there spluttering and shouting. They couldn't see either Bruno or me and they were wondering what all the fuss was about.

"By the way," my grandmother said, "would you like to know who did this to him?" There was a mischievous little smile on her face and I could see that she was about to get Mr Jenkins into trouble.

"Who?" he cried. "Who did it?"

"That woman over there," my grandmother said. "The small one in a black dress at the head of the long table."

"She's RSPCC!" cried Mr Jenkins. "She's the Chairwoman!"

"No, she's not," my grandmother said. "She's The Grand High Witch Of All The World."

"You mean *she* did it, that skinny little woman over there!" shouted Mr Jenkins, pointing at her with a long finger. "By gad, I'll have my lawyers on to her for this! I'll make her pay through the nose!"

"I wouldn't do anything rash," my grandmother said to him. "That woman has magic powers. She might decide to turn *you* into something even sillier than a mouse. A cockroach perhaps."

"Turn *me* into a *cockroach*!" shouted Mr Jenkins, puffing out his chest. "I'd like to see her try!" He swung around and started marching across the Dining-Room towards The Grand High Witch's table. My grandmother and I watched him. Bruno had jumped up on to our table and was also watching his father. Practically everyone in the Dining-Room was watching Mr Jenkins now. I stayed where I was, peeping out of my grandmother's handbag. I thought it might be wiser to stay put.

The Triumph

Mr Jenkins had not gone more than a few paces towards The Grand High Witch's table when a piercing scream rose high above all the other noises in the room, and at the same moment I saw The Grand High Witch go shooting up into the air!

Now she was standing on her chair, still screaming . . .

Now she was on the table-top, waving her arms . . .

"What on earth's happening, Grandmamma?"

"Wait!" my grandmother said. "Keep quiet and watch."

Suddenly all the other witches, more than eighty of them, were beginning to scream and jump up out of their seats as though spikes were being stuck into their bottoms. Some were standing on chairs, some were up on the tables and all of them were wiggling about and waving their arms in the most extraordinary manner.

Then, all at once, they became quiet.

Then they stiffened. Every single witch stood there as stiff and silent as a corpse.

The whole room became deathly still.

"They're shrinking, Grandmamma!" I said. "They're shrinking just like I did!"

"I know they are," my grandmother said.

"It's the Mouse-Maker!" I cried. "Look! Some of them are growing fur on their faces! Why is it working so quickly, Grandmamma?"

"I'll tell you why," my grandmother said. "Because all of them have had massive overdoses, just like you. It's thrown the alarm-clock right out of whack!"

Everyone in the Dining-Room was standing up now to get a better view. People were moving closer. They were beginning to crowd round the two long tables. My grandmother lifted Bruno and me up so that we wouldn't miss any of the fun. In her excitement, she jumped up on to her chair so that she could see over the heads of the crowd.

In another few seconds, all the witches had completely disappeared and the tops of the two long tables were swarming with small brown mice.

All over the Dining-Room women were screaming and strong men were turning white in the face and shouting, "It's crazy! This can't happen! Let's get the heck out of here quick!" Waiters were attacking the mice with chairs and wine-bottles and anything else that came to hand. I saw a chef in a tall white hat rushing out from the kitchen brandishing a frying-pan, and another one just behind *him* was wielding a carving-knife above his head, and everyone was yelling, "Mice! Mice! Mice! We must get rid of the mice!" Only the children in the room were really enjoying it. They all seemed to know instinctively that something good was going on right there in front of them, and they were clapping and cheering and laughing like mad.

"It's time to go," my grandmother said. "Our work is done." She got down off her chair and picked up her handbag and slung it over her arm.

She had me in her right hand and Bruno in her left. "Bruno," she said, "the time has come to restore you to the famous bosom of your family."

"My mum's not very crazy about mice," Bruno said.

"So I noticed," my grandmother said. "She'll just have to get used to you, won't she?"

It was not difficult to find Mr and Mrs Jenkins. You could hear Mrs Jenkins's shrill voice all over the room. "Herbert!" it was screaming. "Herbert, get me out of here! There's mice everywhere! They'll go up my skirts!" She had her arms high up around her husband and from where I was she seemed to be swinging from his neck.

My grandmother advanced upon them and thrust Bruno into Mr Jenkins's hand. "Here's your little boy," she said. "He needs to go on a diet."

"Hi, Dad!" Bruno said. "Hi, Mum!"

Mrs Jenkins screamed even louder. My grandmother, with me in her hand, turned and marched out of the room. She went straight across the hotel lobby and out through the front entrance into the open air.

Outside it was a lovely warm evening and I could hear the waves breaking on the beach just across the road from the hotel.

"Is there a taxi here?" my grandmother said to the tall doorman in his green uniform.

"Certainly, madam," he said, and he put two fingers into his mouth and blew a long shrill whistle. I watched him with envy. For weeks I had been trying to whistle like that but I hadn't succeeded once. Now I never would.

The taxi came. The driver was an oldish man with a thick black drooping moustache. The moustache hung over his mouth like the roots of some plant. "Where to, madam?" he asked. Suddenly, he caught sight of me, a little mouse, nestling in my grandmother's hand. "Blimey!" he said. "What's that?"

"It's my grandson," my grandmother said. "Drive us to the station, please."

"I always liked mice," the old taxi-driver said. "I used to keep 'undreds of 'em when I was a boy.

Mice is the fastest breeders in the world, did you know that, ma'am? So if 'ee's your grandson, then I reckon you'll be having a few *great* grandsons to go with 'im in a couple of weeks' time!"

"Drive us to the station, please," my grandmother said, looking prim.

"Yes, ma'am," he said. "Right away."

My grandmother got into the back of the taxi and sat down and put me on her lap.

"Are we going home?" I asked her.

"Yes," she answered. "Back to Norway."

"Hooray!" I cried. "Oh, hooray, hooray, hooray!"

"I thought you'd like that," she said.

"But what about our luggage?"

"Who cares about luggage?" she said.

The taxi was driving through the streets of Bournemouth and this was the time of day when the pavements were crowded with holiday-makers all wandering about aimlessly with nothing to do.

"How are you feeling, my darling?" my grandmother said.

"Fine," I said. "Quite marvellous."

She began stroking the fur on the back of my neck with one finger. "We have accomplished great feats today," she said.

"It's been terrific," I said. "Absolutely terrific."

The Heart of a Mouse

It was lovely to be back in Norway once again in my grandmother's fine old house. But now that I was so small, everything looked different and it took me quite a while to find my way around. Mine was a world of carpets and table-legs and chair-legs and the little crannies behind large pieces of furniture. A closed door could not be opened and nothing could be reached that was on a table.

But after a few days, my grandmother began to invent gadgets for me in order to make life a bit easier. She got a carpenter to put together a number of slim tall stepladders and she placed one of these against each table in the house so that I could climb up whenever I wanted to. She herself invented a wonderful door-opening device made out of wires and springs and pulleys, with heavy weights dangling on cords, and soon every door in the house had a door-opener on it. All I had to do was to press my front paws on to a tiny wooden platform and hey presto, a spring would stretch and a weight would drop and the door would swing open.

Next, she rigged up an equally ingenious system whereby I could switch on the light whenever I entered a room at night. I cannot explain how it

worked because I know nothing about electricity, but there was a little button let into the floor near the door in every room in the house, and when I pressed the button gently with one paw, the light would come on. When I pressed it a second time, the light would go off again.

My grandmother made me a tiny toothbrush, using a matchstick for the handle, and into this she stuck little bits of bristle that she had snipped off one of her hairbrushes. "You *must* not get any holes in your teeth," she said. "I can't take a *mouse* to a dentist! He'd think I was crazy!"

"It's funny," I said, "but ever since I became a mouse I've hated the taste of sweets and chocolate. So I don't think I'll get any holes."

"You are still going to brush your teeth after every meal," my grandmother said. And I did.

For a bath-tub she gave me a silver sugar-basin, and I bathed in it every night before going to bed. She allowed no one else into the house, not even a servant or a cook. We kept entirely to ourselves and we were very happy in each other's company.

One evening, as I lay on my grandmother's lap in front of the fire, she said to me, "I wonder what happened to that little Bruno."

"I wouldn't be surprised if his father gave him to the hall-porter to drown in the fire-bucket," I answered.

"I'm afraid you may be right," my grandmother said. "The poor little thing."

We were silent for a few minutes, my grandmother puffing away at her black cigar while I dozed comfortably in the warmth.

"Can I ask you something, Grandmamma?" I said.

"Ask me anything you like, my darling."

"How long does a mouse live?"

"Ah," she said. "I've been waiting for you to ask me that."

There was a silence. She sat there smoking away and gazing at the fire.

"Well," I said. "How long *do* we live, us mice?"

"I have been reading about mice," she said. "I have been trying to find out everything I can about them."

"Go on then, Grandmamma. Why don't you tell me?"

"If you really want to know," she said, "I'm afraid a mouse doesn't live for a very long time."

"How long?" I asked.

"Well, an *ordinary* mouse only lives for about three years," she said. "But you are not an ordinary mouse. You are a mouse-person, and that is a very different matter."

"How different?" I asked. "How long does a mouse-person live, Grandmamma?"

"Longer," she said. "Much longer."

"How much longer?" I asked.

"A mouse-person will almost certainly live for three times as long as an ordinary mouse," my grandmother said. "About nine years."

"Good!" I cried. "That's great! It's the best news I've ever had!"

"Why do you say that?" she asked, surprised.

"Because I would never want to live longer than you," I said. "I couldn't stand being looked after by anybody else."

There was a short silence. She had a way of fondling me behind the ears with the tip of one finger. It felt lovely.

"How old are *you*, Grandmamma?" I asked.

"I'm eighty-six," she said.

"Will you live another eight or nine years?"

"I might," she said. "With a bit of luck."

"You've got to," I said. "Because by then I'll be a very old mouse and you'll be a very old grandmother and soon after that we'll both die together."

"That would be perfect," she said.

I had a little doze after that. I just shut my eyes and thought of nothing and felt at peace with the world.

"Would you like me to tell you something about yourself that is very interesting?" my grandmother said.

"Yes please, Grandmamma," I said, without opening my eyes.

"I couldn't believe it at first, but apparently it's quite true," she said.

"What is it?" I asked.

"The heart of a mouse," she said, "and that means *your* heart, is beating at the rate of *five hundred times a minute*! Isn't that amazing?"

"That's not possible," I said, opening my eyes wide.

"It's as true as I'm sitting here," she said. "It's a sort of a miracle."

"That's nearly nine beats every second!" I cried, working it out in my head.

"Correct," she said. "Your heart is going so fast it's impossible to hear the separate beats. All one hears is a soft humming sound."

She was wearing a lace dress and the lace kept tickling my nose. I had to rest my head on my front paws.

"Have *you* ever heard my heart humming away, Grandmamma?" I asked her.

"Often," she said. "I hear it when you are lying very close to me on the pillow at night."

The two of us remained silent in front of the fire for a long time after that, thinking about these wonderful things.

"My darling," she said at last, "are you sure you don't mind being a mouse for the rest of your life?"

"I don't mind at all," I said. "It doesn't matter who you are or what you look like so long as somebody loves you."

It's Off to Work We Go!

For supper that evening my grandmother had a plain omelette and one slice of bread. I had a piece of that brown Norwegian goats' milk cheese known as *gjetost* which I had loved even when I was a boy. We ate in front of the fire, my grandmother in her armchair and me on the table with my cheese on a small plate.

"Grandmamma," I said, "now that we have done away with The Grand High Witch, will all the other witches in the world gradually disappear?"

"I'm quite sure they won't," she answered.

I stopped chewing and stared at her. "But they *must*!" I cried. "Surely they must!"

"I'm afraid not," she said.

"But if she's not there any longer how are they going to get all the money they need? And who is going to give them orders and jazz them up at the Annual Meetings and invent all their magic formulas for them?"

"When a queen bee dies, there is always another queen in the hive ready to take her place," my grandmother said. "It's the same with witches. In the great Headquarters where The Grand High Witch lives, there is always another Grand High Witch waiting in the wings to take over should anything happen."

"Oh no!" I cried. "That means everything we did was for nothing! Have I become a mouse for nothing at all?"

"We saved the children of England," she said. "I don't call that nothing."

"I know, I know!" I cried. "But that's not nearly good enough! I felt sure that all the witches of the world would slowly fade away after we had got rid of their leader! Now you tell me that everything is going to go on just the same as before!"

"Not exactly as before," my grandmother said. "For instance, there are no longer any witches in England. That's quite a triumph, isn't it?"

"But what about the rest of the world?" I cried. "What about America and France and Holland and Germany? And what about Norway?"

"You must not think I have been sitting back and doing nothing these last few days," she said. "I have been giving a great deal of thought and time to that particular problem."

I was looking up at her face when she said this, and all at once I noticed that a little secret smile was beginning to spread slowly around her eyes and the corners of her mouth. "Why are you smiling, Grandmamma?" I asked her.

"I have some rather interesting news for you," she said.

"What news?"

"Shall I tell it to you right from the beginning?"

"Yes please," I said. "I like good news."

She had finished her omelette, and I had had enough of my cheese. She wiped her lips with a napkin and said, "As soon as we arrived back in Norway, I picked up the telephone and made a call to England."

"Who in England, Grandmamma?"

"To the Chief of Police in Bournemouth, my darling. I told him I was the Chief of Police for the whole of Norway and that I was interested in the peculiar happenings that had taken place recently in the Hotel Magnificent."

"Now hang on a sec, Grandmamma," I said. "There's no way an English policeman is going to believe that *you* are the Head of the Norwegian Police."

"I am very good at imitating a man's voice," she

said. "Of course he believed me. The policeman in Bournemouth was honoured to get a call from the Chief of Police for the whole of Norway."

"So what did you ask him?"

"I asked him for the name and address of the lady who had been living in Room 454 in the Hotel Magnificent, the one who disappeared."

"You mean The Grand High Witch!" I cried.

"Yes, my darling."

"And did he give it to you?"

"Naturally he gave it to me. One policeman will always help another policeman."

"By golly, you've got a nerve, Grandmamma!"

"I wanted her address," my grandmother said.

"But did he *know* her address?"

"He did indeed. They had found her passport in her room and her address was in it. It was also in the hotel register. Everyone who stays in an hotel has to put a name and address in the book."

"But surely The Grand High Witch wouldn't have put her *real* name and address in the hotel register?" I said.

"Why ever not?" my grandmother said. "Nobody in the world had the faintest idea who she was except the other witches. Wherever she went, people simply knew her as a nice lady. *You,* my darling, and *you alone,* were the only non-witch ever to see her with her mask off. Even in her home district, in the village where she lived, people knew her as a kindly and very wealthy Baroness who gave large sums of money to charity. I have checked up on that."

205

I was getting excited now. "And that address you got, Grandmamma, that must have been the secret Headquarters of The Grand High Witch."

"It still is," my grandmother said. "And that will be where the new Grand High Witch is certain to be living at this very moment with her retinue of special Assistant Witches. Important rulers are always surrounded by a large retinue of assistants."

"Where is her Headquarters, Grandmamma?" I cried. "Tell me quick where it is!"

"It is a Castle," my grandmother said. "And the fascinating thing is that in that Castle will be all the names and addresses of all the witches in the world! How else could a Grand High Witch run her business? How else could she summon the witches of the various countries to their Annual Meetings?"

"Where is the Castle, Grandmamma?" I cried impatiently. "Which country? Tell me quick!"

"Guess," she said.

"Norway!" I cried.

"Right first time!" she answered. "High up in the mountains above a small village."

This was thrilling news. I did a little dance of excitement on the table-top. My grandmother was getting pretty worked up herself and now she heaved herself out of her chair and began pacing up and down the room, thumping the carpet with her stick.

"So we have work to do, you and I!" she cried out. "We have a great task ahead of us! Thank

heavens you are a mouse! A mouse can go anywhere! All I'll have to do is put you down somewhere near The Grand High Witch's Castle and
you will very easily be able to get inside it and
creep around looking and listening to your heart's
content!"

"I will! I will!" I answered. "No one will ever
see me! Moving about in a big Castle will be
child's play compared with going into a crowded
kitchen full of cooks and waiters!"

"You could spend *days* in there if necessary!"
my grandmother cried. In her excitement she was
waving her stick all over the place, and suddenly
she knocked over a tall and very beautiful vase
that went crashing on to the floor and smashed
into a million pieces. "Forget it," she said. "It's
only Ming. You could spend *weeks* in that Castle
if you wanted to and they'd never know you were
there! I myself would get a room in the village and
you could sneak out of the Castle and have supper
with me every night and tell me what was going
on."

"I could! I could!" I cried out. "And inside the Castle I could go snooping around simply everywhere!"

"But your main job, of course," my grandmother said, "would be to destroy every witch in the place. That really *would* be the end of the whole organisation!"

"*Me* destroy *them*?" I cried. "How could I do that?"

"Can't you guess?" she said.

"Tell me," I said.

"Mouse-Maker!" my grandmother shouted. "Formula 86 Delayed Action Mouse-Maker all over again! You will feed it to everyone in the Castle by putting drops of it into their food! You do remember the recipe, don't you?"

"Every bit of it!" I answered. "You mean we're going to make it ourselves?"

"Why not?" she cried. "If *they* can make it, so can we! It's just a question of knowing what goes into it!"

"Who's going to climb up the tall trees to get the gruntles' eggs?" I asked her.

"I will!" she cried. "I'll do it myself! There's plenty of life in this old dog yet!"

"I think I'd better do that part of it, Grandmamma. You might come a cropper."

"Those are just details!" she cried, waving her stick again. "We shall let nothing stand in our way!"

"And what happens after that?" I asked her. "After the new Grand High Witch and everyone else in the Castle have been turned into mice?"

"Then the Castle will be completely empty and I shall come in and join you and . . ."

"Wait!" I cried. "Hold on, Grandmamma! I've just had a nasty thought!"

"What nasty thought?" she said.

"When the Mouse-Maker turned *me* into a mouse," I said, "I didn't become just any old ordinary mouse that you catch with mouse-traps. I became a talking thinking intelligent mouse-person who wouldn't go *near* a mouse-trap!"

My grandmother stopped dead in her tracks. She already knew what was coming next.

"Therefore," I went on, "if we use the Mouse-Maker to turn the new Grand High Witch and all the other witches in the Castle into mice, the whole place will be swarming with very clever, very nasty, very dangerous talking thinking mouse-witches! They'll all be witches in mouse's clothing. And that", I added, "could be very horrible indeed."

"By golly, you're right!" she cried. "That never occurred to me!"

"I couldn't possibly take on a castleful of mouse-witches," I said.

"Nor could I," she said. "They'd have to be got rid of at once. They'd have to be smashed and bashed and chopped up into little pieces exactly as they were in the Hotel Magnificent."

"I'm not doing that," I said. "I couldn't anyway. I don't think you could either, Grandmamma. And mouse-traps wouldn't be the slightest use. By the way," I added, "The Grand High Witch who did me in was wrong about mouse-traps wasn't she?"

"Yes, yes," my grandmother said impatiently. "But I'm not concerned with *that* Grand High Witch. She's been chopped up long ago by the hotel chef. It's the *new* Grand High Witch we've got to deal with now, the one up in the Castle, and all her assistants. A Grand High Witch is bad enough when she's disguised as a lady, but just think of what she could do if she were a mouse! She could go anywhere!"

"I've got it!" I shouted, leaping about a foot in the air. "I've got the answer!"

"Tell me!" my grandmother snapped.

"The answer is CATS!" I shouted. "Bring on the cats!"

My grandmother stared at me. Then a great grin spread over her face and she shouted, "It's brilliant! Absolutely brilliant!"

"Shove half-a-dozen cats into that Castle," I cried, "and they'll kill every mouse in the place in five minutes, I don't care how clever they are!"

"You're a magician!" my grandmother shouted, starting to wave her stick about once again.

"Look out for the vases, Grandmamma!"

"To heck with the vases!" she shouted. "I'm so thrilled I don't care if I break the lot!"

"Just one thing," I said. "You've got to make absolutely sure I'm well out of the way myself before you put the cats in."

"That's a promise," she said.

210

"What will we do after the cats have killed all the mice?" I asked her.

"I'll take all the cats back to the village and then you and I will have the Castle completely to ourselves."

"And then?" I said.

"Then we shall go through the records and get the names and addresses of all the witches in the whole wide world!"

"And after that?" I said, quivering with excitement.

"After that, my darling, the greatest task of all will begin for you and me! We shall pack our bags and go travelling all over the world! In every country we visit, we shall seek out the houses where the witches are living! We shall find each house, one by one, and having found it, you will creep inside and leave your little drops of deadly Mouse-Maker in the bread, or the cornflakes, or the rice-pudding or whatever food you see lying about. It will be a triumph, my darling! A colossal unbeatable triumph. We shall do it entirely by ourselves, just you and me! That will be our work for the rest of our lives!"

My grandmother picked me up off the table and kissed me on the nose. "Oh, my goodness me, we're going to be busy these next few weeks and months and years!" she cried.

"I think we are," I said. "But what fun and excitement it's going to be!"

"You can say that again!" my grandmother cried, giving me another kiss. "I can't wait to get started!"

Roald Dahl

ESIO TROT

Illustrations by Quentin Blake

to Clover and Luke

Author's Note

Some years ago, when my own children were small, we usually kept a tortoise or two in the garden. In those days, a pet tortoise was a common sight crawling about on the family lawn or in the back yard. You could buy them quite cheaply in any pet-shop and they were probably the least troublesome of all childhood pets, and quite harmless.

Tortoises used to be brought into England by the thousand, packed in crates, and they came mostly from North Africa. But not many years ago a law was passed that made it illegal to bring any tortoises into the country. This was not done to protect us. The little tortoise was not a danger to anybody. It was done purely out of kindness to the tortoise itself. You see, the traders who brought them in used to cram hundreds of them tightly into the packing-crates without food or water and in such horrible conditions that a great many of them always died on the sea-journey over. So rather than allow this cruelty to go on, the Government stopped the whole business.

The things you are going to read about in this story all happened in the days when anyone could go out and buy a nice little tortoise from a pet-shop.

ESIO TROT

Mr Hoppy lived in a small flat high up in a tall concrete building. He lived alone. He had always been a lonely man and now that he was retired from work he was more lonely than ever.

There were two loves in Mr Hoppy's life. One was the flowers he grew on his balcony. They grew in pots and tubs and baskets, and in summer the little balcony became a riot of colour.

Mr Hoppy's second love was a secret he kept entirely to himself.

The balcony immediately below Mr Hoppy's jutted out a good bit further from the building than his own, so Mr Hoppy always had a fine view of what was going on down there. This balcony belonged to an attractive middle-aged lady called Mrs Silver. Mrs Silver was a widow who also lived alone. And although she didn't know it, it was she who was the object of Mr Hoppy's secret love. He had loved her from his balcony for many years, but he was a very shy man and he had never been able to bring himself to give her even the smallest hint of his love.

Every morning, Mr Hoppy and Mrs Silver exchanged polite conversation, the one looking down from above, the other looking up, but that was as far as it ever went. The distance between their balconies might not have been more than a few yards, but to Mr Hoppy it seemed like a million miles. He longed to invite Mrs Silver up for a cup of tea and a biscuit, but every time he was about to form the words on his lips, his courage failed him. As I said, he was a very very shy man.

Oh, if only, he kept telling himself, if only he could do something tremendous like saving her life or rescuing her from a gang of armed thugs, if only he could perform some great feat that would make him a hero in her eyes. If only. . .

The trouble with Mrs Silver was that she gave all her love to somebody else, and that somebody was a small tortoise called Alfie. Every day, when Mr Hoppy looked over his balcony and saw Mrs Silver whispering endearments to Alfie and stroking his shell, he felt absurdly jealous. He wouldn't even have minded becoming a tortoise himself if it meant Mrs Silver stroking his shell each morning and whispering endearments to him.

Alfie had been with Mrs Silver for years and he lived on her balcony summer and winter. Planks had been placed around the sides of the balcony so that Alfie could walk about without toppling over the edge, and in one corner there was a little house into which Alfie would crawl every night to keep warm.

When the colder weather came along in November, Mrs Silver would fill Alfie's house

with dry hay, and the tortoise would crawl in
there and bury himself deep under the hay and
go to sleep for months on end without food or
water. This is called hibernating.

In early spring, when Alfie felt the warmer
weather through his shell, he would wake up
and crawl very slowly out of his house on to the
balcony. And Mrs Silver would clap her hands
with joy and cry out, "Welcome back, my
darling one! Oh, how I have missed you!"

It was at times like these that Mr Hoppy
wished more than ever that he could change
places with Alfie and become a tortoise.

Now we come to a certain bright
morning in May when something
happened that changed and indeed
electrified Mr Hoppy's life. He was
leaning over his balcony-rail watching
Mrs Silver serving Alfie his breakfast.

"Here's the heart of the lettuce for you,
my lovely," she was saying. "And here's a
slice of fresh tomato and a piece of crispy
celery."

"Good morning, Mrs Silver," Mr Hoppy
said. "Alfie's looking well this morning."

"Isn't he gorgeous!" Mrs Silver said, looking
up and beaming at him.

"Absolutely gorgeous," Mr Hoppy said, not meaning it. And now, as he looked down at Mrs Silver's smiling face gazing up into his own, he thought for the thousandth time how pretty she was, how sweet and gentle and full of kindness, and his heart ached with love.

"I do so wish he would *grow* a little faster,"
Mrs Silver was saying. "Every spring, when he
wakes up from his winter sleep, I weigh him on
the kitchen scales. And do you know that in all
the eleven years I've had him he's not gained
more than *three ounces*! That's almost *nothing*!"

"What does he weigh now?" Mr Hoppy asked
her.

"Just thirteen ounces," Mrs Silver answered.
"About as much as a grapefruit."

"Yes, well, tortoises are very slow growers,"
Mr Hoppy said solemnly. "But they can live for a
hundred years."

"I know that," Mrs Silver said. "But I do so
wish he would grow just a little bit bigger. He's
such a tiny wee fellow."

"He seems just fine as he is," Mr Hoppy said.

"No, he's *not* just fine!" Mrs Silver cried. "Try

to think how miserable it must make him feel to be so titchy! Everyone wants to grow up."

"You really *would* love him to grow bigger, wouldn't you?" Mr Hoppy said, and even as he said it his mind suddenly went *click* and an amazing idea came rushing into his head.

"Of course I would!" Mrs Silver cried. "I'd give *anything* to make it happen! Why, I've seen pictures of giant tortoises that are so huge people can ride on their backs! If Alfie were to see those he'd turn green with envy!"

Mr Hoppy's mind was spinning like a fly-wheel. Here, surely, was his big chance! Grab it, he told himself. Grab it quick!

"Mrs Silver," he said. "I do actually happen to know how to make tortoises grow faster, if that's really what you want."

"You do?" she cried. "Oh, please tell me! Am I feeding him the wrong things?"

"I worked in North Africa once," Mr Hoppy said. "That's where all these tortoises in England come from, and a bedouin tribesman told me the secret."

"Tell me!" cried Mrs Silver. "I beg you to tell me, Mr Hoppy! I'll be your slave for life."

When he heard the words *your slave for life*, a little shiver of excitement swept through Mr Hoppy. "Wait there," he said. "I'll have to go in and write something down for you."

In a couple of minutes Mr Hoppy was back on the balcony with a sheet of paper in his hand. "I'm going to lower it to you on a bit of string," he said, "or it might blow away. Here it comes."

Mrs Silver caught the paper and held it up in front of her. This is what she read:

ESIO TROT, ESIO TROT,
TEG REGGIB REGGIB!
EMOC NO, ESIO TROT,
WORG PU, FFUP PU, TOOHS PU!
GNIRPS PU, WOLB PU, LLEWS PU!
EGROG! ELZZUG! FFUTS! PLUG!
TUP NO TAF, ESIO TROT, TUP NO TAF!
TEG NO, TEG NO! ELBBOG DOOF!

"What *does* it mean?" she asked. "Is it another language?"

"It's tortoise language," Mr Hoppy said. "Tortoises are very backward creatures. Therefore they can only understand words that are written backwards. That's obvious, isn't it?"

"I suppose so," Mrs Silver said, bewildered.

"Esio trot is simply tortoise spelled backwards," Mr Hoppy said. "Look at it."

"So it is," Mrs Silver said.

"The other words are spelled backwards, too," Mr Hoppy said. "If you turn them round into human language, they simply say:

TORTOISE, TORTOISE,
GET BIGGER BIGGER!
COME ON, TORTOISE,
GROW UP, PUFF UP, SHOOT UP!
SPRING UP, BLOW UP, SWELL UP!
GORGE! GUZZLE! STUFF! GULP!
PUT ON FAT, TORTOISE, PUT ON FAT!
GET ON, GET ON! GOBBLE FOOD!"

Mrs Silver examined the magic words on the paper more closely. "I guess you're right," she said. "How clever. But there's an awful lot of poos in it. Are they something special?"

"Poo is a very strong word in any language," Mr Hoppy said, "especially with tortoises. Now what you have to do, Mrs Silver, is hold Alfie up to your face and whisper these words to him three times a day, morning, noon and night. Let me hear you practice them."

Very slowly and stumbling a little over the strange words, Mrs Silver read the whole message out loud in tortoise language.

"Not bad," Mr Hoppy said. "But try to get a little more expression into it when you say it to Alfie. If you do it properly I'll bet you anything you like that in a few months' time he'll be twice as big as he is now."

"I'll try it," Mrs Silver said. "I'll try anything. Of course I will. But I can't believe it'll work."

"You wait and see," Mr Hoppy said, smiling at her.

Back in his flat, Mr Hoppy was simply quivering all over with excitement. *Your slave for life*, he kept repeating to himself. What bliss!

But there was a lot of work to be done before that happened.

236

The only furniture in Mr Hoppy's small living-room was a table and two chairs. These he moved into his bedroom. Then he went out and bought a sheet of thick canvas and spread it over the entire living-room floor to protect his carpet.

Next, he got out the telephone-book and wrote down the address of every pet-shop in the city. There were fourteen of them altogether.

It took him two days to visit each pet-shop and choose his tortoises. He wanted a great many, at least one hundred, perhaps more. And he had to choose them very carefully.

To you and me there is not much difference between one tortoise and another. They differ only in their size and in the colour of their shells. Alfie had a darkish shell, so Mr Hoppy chose only the darker-shelled tortoises for his great collection.

Size, of course, was everything. Mr Hoppy chose all sorts of different sizes, some weighing only slightly more than Alfie's thirteen ounces, others a great deal more, but he didn't want any that weighed less.

"Feed them cabbage leaves," the pet-shop owners told him. "That's all they'll need. And a bowl of water."

When he had finished, Mr Hoppy, in his
enthusiasm, had bought no less than one
hundred and forty tortoises and he carried them
home in baskets, ten or fifteen at a time. He had
to make a lot of trips and he was quite exhausted
at the end of it all, but it was worth it. Boy, was it
worth it! And what an amazing sight his living-
room was when they were all in there together!
The floor was swarming with tortoises of

different sizes, some walking slowly about and exploring, some munching cabbage leaves, others drinking water from a big shallow dish. They made just the faintest rustling sound as they moved over the canvas sheet, but that was all. Mr Hoppy had to pick his way carefully on his toes between this moving sea of brown shells whenever he walked across the room. But enough of that. He must get on with the job.

Before he retired Mr Hoppy had been a mechanic in a bus-garage. And now he went back to his old place of work and asked his mates if he might use his old bench for an hour or two.

What he had to do now was to make something that would reach down from his own balcony to Mrs Silver's balcony and pick up a tortoise. This was not difficult for a mechanic like Mr Hoppy.

First he made two metal claws or fingers, and these he attached to the end of a long metal tube. He ran two stiff wires down inside the tube and connected them to the metal claws in such a way that when you pulled the wires, the claws closed, and when you pushed them, the claws opened. The wires were joined to a handle at the other end of the tube. It was all very simple.

Mr Hoppy was ready to begin.

Mrs Silver had a part-time job. She worked from noon until five o'clock every weekday afternoon in a shop that sold newspapers and sweets. That made things a lot easier for Mr Hoppy.

So on that first exciting afternoon, after he had made sure that Mrs Silver had gone to work, Mr Hoppy went out on to his balcony armed with his long metal pole. He called this his tortoise-catcher. He leaned over the balcony railings and lowered the pole down on to Mrs Silver's balcony below. Alfie was basking in the pale sunlight over to one side.

"Hello Alfie," Mr Hoppy said. "You are about to go for a little ride."

He wiggled the tortoise-catcher till it was right above Alfie. He pushed the hand-lever so that the claws opened wide. Then he lowered the two claws neatly over Alfie's shell and pulled the lever. The claws closed tightly over the shell like two fingers of a hand. He hauled Alfie up on to his own balcony. It was easy.

Mr Hoppy weighed Alfie on his own kitchen scales just to make sure that Mrs Silver's figure of thirteen ounces was correct. It was.

Now, holding Alfie in one hand, he picked his way carefully through his huge collection of tortoises to find one that first of all had the same colour shell as Alfie's and secondly weighed *exactly two ounces more.*

Two ounces is not much. It is less than a smallish hen's egg weighs. But you see, the important thing in Mr Hoppy's plan was to make sure that the new tortoise was bigger than Alfie but only a *tiny bit* bigger. The difference had to be so small that Mrs Silver wouldn't notice it.

From his vast collection, it was not difficult for Mr Hoppy to find just the tortoise he wanted. He wanted one that weighed fifteen ounces exactly on his kitchen scales, no more and no less. When he had got it, he put it on the kitchen table beside Alfie, and even he could hardly tell that one was bigger than the other. But it *was* bigger. It was bigger by two ounces. This was Tortoise Number 2.

Mr Hoppy took Tortoise Number 2 out on to the balcony and gripped it in the claws of his tortoise-catcher. Then he lowered it on to Mrs Silver's balcony, right beside a nice fresh lettuce leaf.

Tortoise Number 2 had never eaten tender juicy lettuce leaves before. It had only had thick old cabbage leaves. It loved the lettuce and started chomping away at it with great gusto.

There followed a rather nervous two hours' wait for Mrs Silver to return from work.

Would she see any difference between the new tortoise and Alfie? It was going to be a tense moment.

Out on to her balcony swept Mrs Silver.

"Alfie, my darling!" she cried out. "Mummy's back! Have you missed me?"

Mr Hoppy, peering over his railing, but well hidden between two huge potted plants, held his breath.

The new tortoise was still chomping away at the lettuce.

"My my, Alfie, you do seem hungry today," Mrs Silver was saying. "It must be Mr Hoppy's magic words I've been whispering to you."

Mr Hoppy watched as Mrs Silver picked the tortoise up and stroked his shell. Then she fished Mr Hoppy's piece of paper out of her pocket, and holding the tortoise very close to her face, she whispered, reading from the paper:

"ESIO TROT, ESIO TROT,
TEG REGGIB REGGIB!
EMOC NO, ESIO TROT,
WORG PU, FFUP PU, TOOHS PU!
GNIRPS PU, WOLB PU, LLEWS PU!
EGROG! ELZZUG! FFUTS! PLUG!
TUP NO TAF, ESIO TROT, TUP NO TAF!
TEG NO, TEG NO! ELBBOG DOOF!"

Mr Hoppy popped his head out of the foliage and called out, "Good evening, Mrs Silver. How is Alfie tonight?"

"Oh, he's lovely," Mrs Silver said, looking up and beaming. "And he's developing *such* an appetite! I've never seen him eat like this before! It must be the magic words."

"You never know," Mr Hoppy said darkly. "You never know."

Mr Hoppy waited seven whole days before he made his next move.

On the afternoon of the seventh day, when Mrs Silver was at work, he lifted Tortoise Number 2 from the balcony below and brought it into his living-room. Number 2 had weighed exactly *fifteen* ounces. He must now find one that weighed exactly *seventeen* ounces, two ounces more.

From his enormous collection, he easily found a seventeen-ounce tortoise and once again he made sure the shells matched in colour. Then he lowered Tortoise Number 3 on to Mrs Silver's balcony.

As you will have guessed by now, Mr Hoppy's secret was a very simple one. If a creature grows slowly enough – I mean very very slowly indeed – then you'll never notice that it has grown at all, especially if you see it every day.

It's the same with children. They are actually growing taller every week, but their mothers never notice it until they grow out of their clothes.

Slowly does it, Mr Hoppy told himself. Don't hurry it.

So this is how things went over the next eight weeks.

In the beginning

ALFIE   weight 13 ounces

End of first week

TORTOISE NO. 2   weight 15 ounces

End of second week

TORTOISE NO. 3   weight 17 ounces

End of third week

TORTOISE NO. 4   weight 19 ounces

End of fourth week

TORTOISE NO. 5   weight 21 ounces

End of fifth week

TORTOISE NO. 6   weight 23 ounces

TORTOISE NO. 7   weight 25 ounces

End of seventh week

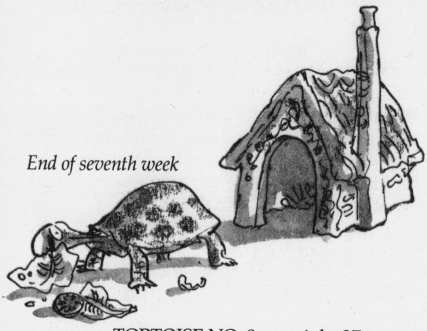

TORTOISE NO. 8   weight 27 ounces

Alfie's weight was thirteen ounces. Tortoise Number 8 was twenty-seven ounces. Very slowly, over seven weeks, Mrs Silver's pet had more than doubled in size and the good lady hadn't noticed a thing.

Even to Mr Hoppy, peering down over his railing, Tortoise Number 8 looked pretty big. It was amazing that Mrs Silver had hardly noticed anything at all during the great operation. Only once had she looked up and said, "You know, Mr Hoppy, I do believe he's getting a bit bigger. What do you think?"

"I can't see a lot of difference myself," Mr Hoppy had answered casually.

But now perhaps it was time to call a halt, and that evening Mr Hoppy was just about to go out and suggest to Mrs Silver that she ought to weigh Alfie when a startled cry from the balcony below brought him outside fast.

"Look!" Mrs Silver was shouting. "Alfie's too big to get through the door of his little house! He must have grown enormously!"

"Weigh him," Mr Hoppy ordered. "Take him in and weigh him quick."

Mrs Silver did just that, and in half a minute she was back holding the tortoise in both hands and waving it above her head and shouting, "Guess what, Mr Hoppy! Guess what! He weighs twenty-seven ounces! He's twice as big as he was before! Oh you darling!" she cried, stroking the tortoise. "Oh, you great big wonderful boy! Just look what clever Mr Hoppy has done for you!"

Mr Hoppy suddenly felt very brave. "Mrs Silver," he said. "Do you think I could pop down to your balcony and hold Alfie myself?"

"Why, of course you can!" Mrs Silver cried. "Come down at once."

Mr Hoppy rushed down the stairs and Mrs Silver opened the door to him. Together they went out on to the balcony. "Just look at him!" Mrs Silver said proudly. "Isn't he grand!"

"He's a big good-sized tortoise now," Mr Hoppy said.

"And *you* did it!" Mrs Silver cried. "You're a miracle-man, you are indeed!"

"But what *am* I going to do about his house?" Mrs Silver said. "He must have a house to go into at night, but now he can't get through the door."

They were standing on the balcony looking at the tortoise who was trying to push his way into his house. But he was too big.

"I shall have to enlarge the door," Mrs Silver said.

"Don't do that," Mr Hoppy said. "You mustn't go chopping up such a pretty little house. After all, he only needs to be just a tiny bit smaller and he could get in easily."

"How can he possibly get smaller?" Mrs Silver asked.

"That's simple," Mr Hoppy said. "Change the

magic words. Instead of telling him to get
bigger and bigger, tell him to get a bit smaller.
But in tortoise language of course."

"Will that work?"

"Of course it'll work."

"Tell me exactly what I have to say, Mr
Hoppy."

Mr Hoppy got out a piece of paper and a pencil and wrote:

ESIO TROT, ESIO TROT,
TEG A TIB RELLAMS, A TIB RELLAMS.

"That'll do it, Mrs Silver," he said, handing her the paper.

"I don't mind trying it," Mrs Silver said. "But look here, I wouldn't want him to get titchy small all over again, Mr Hoppy."

"He won't, dear lady, he won't," Mr Hoppy said. "Say it only tonight and tomorrow morning and then see what happens. We might be lucky."

"If it works," Mrs Silver said, touching him softly on the arm, "then you are the cleverest man alive."

The next afternoon, as soon as Mrs Silver had gone to work, Mr Hoppy lifted the tortoise up from her balcony and carried it inside. All he had to do now was to find one that was a shade smaller, so that it would just go through the door of the little house.

He chose one and lowered it down with his tortoise-catcher. Then, still gripping the tortoise, he tested it to see if it would go through the door. It wouldn't.

He chose another. Again he tested it. This one went through nicely. Good. He placed the tortoise in the middle of the balcony beside a nice piece of lettuce and went inside to await Mrs Silver's homecoming.

That evening, Mr Hoppy was watering his plants on the balcony when suddenly he heard Mrs Silver's shouts from below, shrill with excitement.

"Mr Hoppy! Mr Hoppy! Where are you?" she was shouting. "Just look at this!"

Mr Hoppy popped his head over the railing and said, "What's up?"

"Oh, Mr Hoppy, it's worked!" she was crying. "Your magic words have worked again on Alfie! He can now get through the door of his little house! It's a miracle!"

"Can I come down and look?" Mr Hoppy shouted back.

"Come down at once, my dear man!" Mrs Silver answered. "Come down and see the wonders you have worked upon my darling Alfie!"

Mr
Hoppy
turned and
ran from the
balcony into the
living-room, jumping
on tip-toe like a ballet-
dancer between the sea of
tortoises that covered the floor.
He flung open his front door and
flew down the stairs two at a time with
the love-songs of a thousand cupids ringing
in his ears. *This is it!* he whispered to himself
under his breath. *The greatest moment of my life is
coming up now! I mustn't bish it. I mustn't bosh it! I
must keep very calm!* When he was three-quarters
way down the stairs he caught sight of Mrs
Silver already standing at the open door waiting
to welcome him with a huge smile on her face.
She flung her arms around him and cried out,
"You really are the most wonderful man I've ever
met! You can do anything! Come in at once and
let me make you a cup of tea. That's the very
least you deserve!"

Seated in a comfortable armchair in Mrs
Silver's parlour, sipping his tea, Mr Hoppy was
all of a twitter. He looked at the lovely lady
sitting opposite him and smiled at her. She
smiled right back at him.

267

That smile of hers, so warm and friendly, suddenly gave him the courage he needed, and he said, "Mrs Silver, please will you marry me?"

"Why, Mr Hoppy!" she cried. "I didn't think you'd ever get round to asking me! Of course I'll marry you!"

Mr Hoppy got rid of his teacup and the two of them stood up and embraced warmly in the middle of the room.

"It's all due to Alfie," Mrs Silver said, slightly breathless.

"Good old Alfie," Mr Hoppy said. "We'll keep him for ever."

The next afternoon, Mr Hoppy took all his other tortoises back to the pet-shops and said they could have them for nothing. Then he cleaned up his living-room, leaving not a leaf of cabbage nor a trace of tortoise.

A few weeks later, Mrs Silver became Mrs
Hoppy and the two of them lived very happily
ever after.

P.S. I expect you are wondering what happened to little Alfie, the first of them all. Well, he was bought a week later from one of the pet-shops by a small girl called Roberta Squibb, and he settled down in Roberta's garden. Every day she fed him lettuce and tomato slices and crispy celery, and in the winters he hibernated in a box of dried leaves in the tool-shed.

That was a long time ago. Roberta has grown up and is now married and has two children of her own. She lives in another house, but Alfie is still with her, still the much-loved family pet, and Roberta reckons that by now he must be about thirty years old. It has taken him all that time to grow to twice the size he was when Mrs Silver had him. But he made it in the end.

Roald Dahl

The Twits

Illustrations by Quentin Blake

For Emma

Contents

Hairy Faces

What a lot of hairy-faced men there are around nowadays.

When a man grows hair all over his face it is impossible to tell what he really looks like.

Perhaps that's why he does it. He'd rather you didn't know.

Then there's the problem of washing.

When the very hairy ones wash their faces, it must be as big a job as when you and I wash the hair on our heads.

So what I want to know is this. How often do all these hairy-faced men wash their faces? Is it only once a week, like us, on Sunday nights? And do they shampoo it? Do they use a hair-dryer? Do they rub hair-tonic in to stop their faces from going bald? Do they go to a barber to have their hairy faces cut and trimmed or do they do it themselves in front of the bathroom mirror with nail-scissors?

I don't know. But next time you see a man with a hairy face (which will probably be as soon as you step out on to the street) maybe you will look at him more closely and start wondering about some of these things.

Mr Twit

MR TWIT was one of these very hairy-faced men. The whole of his face except for his forehead, his eyes and his nose, was covered with thick hair. The stuff even sprouted in revolting tufts out of his nostrils and ear-holes.

Mr Twit felt that this hairiness made him look terrifically wise and grand. But in truth he was neither of these things. Mr Twit was a twit. He was born a twit. And now at the age of sixty, he was a bigger twit than ever.

The hair on Mr Twit's face didn't grow smooth and matted as it does on most hairy-faced men. It grew in spikes that stuck out straight like the bristles of a nailbrush.

And how often did Mr Twit wash this bristly nail-brushy face of his?

The answer is NEVER, not even on Sundays.

He hadn't washed it for years.

Dirty Beards

As you know, an ordinary unhairy face like yours or mine simply gets a bit smudgy if it is not washed often enough, and there's nothing so awful about that.

But a hairy face is a very different matter. Things *cling* to hairs, especially food. Things like gravy go right in among the hairs and stay there. You and I can wipe our smooth faces with a flannel and we quickly look more or less all right again, but the hairy man cannot do that.

We can also, if we are careful, eat our meals without spreading food all over our faces. But not so the hairy man. Watch carefully next time you see a hairy man eating his lunch and you will notice that even if he opens his mouth very wide, it is impossible for him to get a spoonful of beef-stew or ice-cream and chocolate sauce into it without leaving some of it on the hairs.

Mr Twit didn't even bother to open his mouth wide when he ate. As a result (and because he never washed) there were always hundreds of bits of old breakfasts and lunches and suppers sticking to the

hairs around his face. They weren't big bits, mind you, because he used to wipe those off with the back of his hand or on his sleeve while he was eating. But if you looked closely (not that you'd ever want to) you would see tiny little specks of dried-up scrambled eggs stuck to the hairs, and spinach and tomato ketchup and fish fingers and minced chicken livers and all the other disgusting things Mr Twit liked to eat.

TINNED SARDINE

CORNFLAKE

STILTON CHEESE

If you looked closer still (hold your noses, ladies and gentlemen), if you peered deep into the moustachy bristles sticking out over his upper lip, you would probably see much larger objects that had escaped the wipe of his hand, things that had been there for months and months, like a piece of maggoty green cheese or a mouldy old cornflake or even the slimy tail of a tinned sardine.

Because of all this, Mr Twit never went really hungry. By sticking out his tongue and curling it sideways to explore the hairy jungle around his mouth, he was always able to find a tasty morsel here and there to nibble on.

What I am trying to tell you is that Mr Twit was a foul and smelly old man.

He was also an extremely horrid old man as you will find out in a moment.

Mrs Twit

MRS TWIT was no better than her husband.

She did not, of course, have a hairy face. It was a pity she didn't because that at any rate would have hidden some of her fearful ugliness.

Take a look at her.

Have you ever seen a woman with an uglier face than that? I doubt it.

But the funny thing is that Mrs Twit wasn't born ugly. She'd had quite a nice face when she was young. The ugliness had grown upon her year by year as she got older.

Why would that happen? I'll tell you why.

If a person has ugly thoughts, it begins to show on the face. And when that person has ugly thoughts every day, every week, every year, the face gets uglier and uglier until it gets so ugly you can hardly bear to look at it.

A person who has good thoughts cannot ever be ugly. You can have a wonky nose and a crooked mouth and a double chin and stick-out teeth, but if you have good thoughts they will shine out of your face like sunbeams and you will always look lovely.

Nothing good shone out of Mrs Twit's face.

In her right hand she carried a walking-stick. She used to tell people that this was because she had warts growing on the sole of her left foot and walking was painful. But the real reason she carried a stick was so that she could hit things with it, things like dogs and cats and small children.

And then there was the glass eye. Mrs Twit had a glass eye that was always looking the other way.

The Glass Eye

You can play a lot of tricks with a glass eye because you can take it out and pop it back in again any time you like. You can bet your life Mrs Twit knew all the tricks.

One morning she took out her glass eye and dropped it into Mr Twit's mug of beer when he wasn't looking.

Mr Twit sat there drinking the beer slowly. The froth made a white ring on the hairs around his mouth. He wiped the white froth on to his sleeve and wiped his sleeve on his trousers.

"You're plotting something," Mrs Twit said, keeping her back turned so he wouldn't see that she had taken out her glass eye. "Whenever you go all quiet like that I know very well you're plotting something."

Mrs Twit was right. Mr Twit was plotting away like mad. He was trying to think up a really nasty trick he could play on his wife that day.

"You'd better be careful," Mrs Twit said, "because when I see you starting to plot, I watch you like a wombat."

"Oh, do shut up, you old hag," Mr Twit said. He went on drinking his beer, and his evil mind kept working away on the latest horrid trick he was going to play on the old woman.

Suddenly, as Mr Twit tipped the last drop of beer down his throat, he caught sight of Mrs Twit's awful glass eye staring up at him from the bottom of the mug. It made him jump.

"I told you I was watching you," cackled Mrs Twit. "I've got eyes everywhere so you'd better be careful."

The Frog

To pay her back for the glass eye in his beer, Mr Twit decided he would put a frog in Mrs Twit's bed.

He caught a big one down by the pond and carried it back secretly in a box.

That night, when Mrs Twit was in the bathroom getting ready for bed, Mr Twit slipped the frog between her sheets. Then he got into his own bed and waited for the fun to begin.

Mrs Twit came back and climbed into her bed and put out the light. She lay there in the dark scratching her tummy. Her tummy was itching. Dirty old hags like her always have itchy tummies.

Then all at once she felt something cold and slimy crawling over her feet. She screamed.

"What's the matter with you?" Mr Twit said.

"Help!" screamed Mrs Twit, bouncing about. "There's something in my bed!"

"I'll bet it's that Giant Skillywiggler I saw on the floor just now," Mr Twit said.

"That *what*?" screamed Mrs Twit.

"I tried to kill it but it got away," Mr Twit said. "It's got teeth like screwdrivers!"

"Help!" screamed Mrs Twit. "Save me! It's all over my feet!"

"It'll bite off your toes," said Mr Twit.

Mrs Twit fainted.

Mr Twit got out of bed and fetched a jug of cold water. He poured the water over Mrs Twit's head to revive her. The frog crawled up from under the sheets to get near the water. It started jumping about on the pillow. Frogs love water. This one was having a good time.

When Mrs Twit came to, the frog had just jumped on to her face. This is not a nice thing to happen to anyone in bed at night. She screamed again.

"By golly it *is* a Giant Skillywiggler!" Mr Twit said. "It'll bite off your nose."

Mrs Twit leapt out of bed and flew downstairs and spent the night on the sofa. The frog went to sleep on her pillow.

The Wormy Spaghetti

The next day, to pay Mr Twit back for the frog trick, Mrs Twit sneaked out into the garden and dug up some worms. She chose big long ones and put them in a tin and carried the tin back to the house under her apron.

At one o'clock, she cooked spaghetti for lunch and she mixed the worms in with the spaghetti, but only on her husband's plate. The worms didn't show because everything was covered with tomato sauce and sprinkled with cheese.

"Hey, my spaghetti's moving!" cried Mr Twit, poking around in it with his fork.

"It's a new kind," Mrs Twit said, taking a mouthful

from her own plate which of course had no worms. "It's called Squiggly Spaghetti. It's delicious. Eat it up while it's nice and hot."

Mr Twit started eating, twisting the long tomato-covered strings around his fork and shovelling them into his mouth. Soon there was tomato sauce all over his hairy chin.

"It's not as good as the ordinary kind," he said, talking with his mouth full. "It's too squishy."

"I find it very tasty," Mrs Twit said. She was watching him from the other end of the table. It gave her great pleasure to watch him eating worms.

"I find it rather bitter," Mr Twit said. "It's got a distinctly bitter flavour. Buy the other kind next time."

Mrs Twit waited until Mr Twit had eaten the whole plateful. Then she said, "You want to know why your spaghetti was squishy?"

Mr Twit wiped the tomato sauce from his beard with a corner of the tablecloth. "Why?" he said.

"And why it had a nasty bitter taste?"

"Why?" he said.

"Because it was *worms*!" cried Mrs Twit, clapping her hands and stamping her feet on the floor and rocking with horrible laughter.

The Funny Walking-stick

To pay Mrs Twit back for the worms in his spaghetti, Mr Twit thought up a really clever nasty trick.

One night, when the old woman was asleep, he crept out of bed and took her walking-stick downstairs to his workshed. There he stuck a tiny round piece of wood (no thicker than a penny) on to the bottom of the stick.

This made the stick longer, but the difference was so small, the next morning Mrs Twit didn't notice it.

The following night, Mr Twit stuck on another tiny bit of wood. Every night, he crept downstairs and added an extra tiny thickness of wood to the end of the walking-stick. He did it very neatly so that the extra bits looked like a part of the old stick.

Gradually, but oh so gradually, Mrs Twit's walking-stick was getting longer and longer.

Now when something is growing very very slowly, it is almost impossible to notice it happening. You yourself, for example, are actually growing taller every day that goes by, but you wouldn't think it, would you? It's happening so slowly you can't even notice it from one week to the next.

It was the same with Mrs Twit's walking-stick. It was all so slow and gradual that she didn't notice how long it was getting even when it was halfway up to her shoulder.

"That stick's too long for you," Mr Twit said to her one day.

"Why so it is!" Mrs Twit said, looking at the stick. "I've had a feeling there was something wrong but I couldn't for the life of me think what it was."

"There's something wrong all right," Mr Twit said, beginning to enjoy himself.

"What *can* have happened?" Mrs Twit said, staring at her old walking-stick. "It must suddenly have grown longer."

"Don't be a fool!" Mr Twit said. "How can a walking-stick possibly grow longer? It's made of dead wood, isn't it? Dead wood can't grow."

"Then what on earth has happened?" cried Mrs Twit.

"It's not the stick, it's *you*!" said Mr Twit, grinning horribly. "It's *you* that's getting *shorter*! I've been noticing it for some time now."

"That's not true!" cried Mrs Twit.

"You're shrinking, woman!" said Mr Twit.

"It's not possible!"

"Oh yes it jolly well is," said Mr Twit. "You're shrinking fast! You're shrinking *dangerously* fast! Why, you must have shrunk at least a foot in the last few days!"

"Never!" she cried.

"Of course you have! Take a look at your stick, you old goat, and see how much you've shrunk in comparison! You've got the *shrinks*, that's what you've got! You've got the dreaded *shrinks*!"

Mrs Twit began to feel so trembly she had to sit down.

Mrs Twit Has the Shrinks

As soon as Mrs Twit sat down, Mr Twit pointed at her and shouted, "There you are! You're sitting in your old chair and you've shrunk so much your feet aren't even touching the ground!"

Mrs Twit looked down at her feet and by golly the man was right. Her feet were not touching the ground.

Mr Twit, you see, had been just as clever with the chair as he'd been with the walking-stick. Every night when he had gone downstairs and stuck a little bit extra on to the stick, he had done the same to the four legs of Mrs Twit's chair.

"Just look at you sitting there in your same old chair," he cried, "and you've shrunk so much your feet are dangling in the air!"

Mrs Twit went white with fear.

"You've got the *shrinks*!" cried Mr Twit, pointing his finger at her like a pistol. "You've got them badly! You've got the most terrible case of shrinks I've ever seen!"

Mrs Twit became so frightened she began to dribble. But Mr Twit, still remembering the worms in his spaghetti, didn't feel sorry for her at all. "I suppose you know what *happens* to you when you get the shrinks?" he said.

"What?" gasped Mrs Twit. "What happens?"

"Your head SHRINKS into your neck . . .

"And your neck SHRINKS into your body . . .

"And your body SHRINKS into your legs . . .

"And your legs SHRINK into your feet. And in the end there's nothing left except a pair of shoes and a bundle of old clothes."

"I can't bear it!" cried Mrs Twit.

"It's a terrible disease," said Mr Twit. "The worst in the world."

"How long have I got?" cried Mrs Twit. "How long before I finish up as a bundle of old clothes and a pair of shoes?"

Mr Twit put on a very solemn face. "At the rate you're going," he said, shaking his head sadly, "I'd say not more than ten or eleven days."

"But isn't there *anything* we can do?" cried Mrs Twit.

"There's only one cure for the shrinks," said Mr Twit.

"Tell me!" she cried. "Oh, tell me quickly!"

"We'll have to hurry!" said Mr Twit.

"I'm ready. I'll hurry! I'll do anything you say!" cried Mrs Twit.

"You won't last long if you don't," said Mr Twit, giving her another grizzly grin.

"What is it I must do?" cried Mrs Twit, clutching her cheeks.

"You've got to be *stretched*," said Mr Twit.

Mrs Twit Gets a Stretching

Mr Twit led Mrs Twit outdoors where he had everything ready for the great stretching.

He had one hundred balloons and lots of string.

He had a gas cylinder for filling the balloons.

He had fixed an iron ring into the ground.

"Stand here," he said, pointing to the iron ring. He then tied Mrs Twit's ankles to the iron ring.

When that was done, he began filling the balloons with gas. Each balloon was on a long string and when it was filled with gas it pulled on its string, trying to go up and up. Mr Twit tied the ends of the strings to the top half of Mrs Twit's body. Some he tied round her neck, some under her arms, some to her wrists and some even to her hair.

Soon there were fifty coloured balloons floating in the air above Mrs Twit's head.

"Can you feel them stretching you?" asked Mr Twit.

"I can! I can!" cried Mrs Twit. "They're stretching me like mad."

He put on another ten balloons. The upward pull became very strong.

Mrs Twit was quite helpless now. With her feet tied to the ground and her arms pulled upwards by the balloons, she was unable to move. She was a prisoner, and Mr Twit had intended to go away and leave her

like that for a couple of days and nights to teach her a lesson. In fact, he was just about to leave when Mrs Twit opened her big mouth and said something silly.

"Are you sure my feet are tied properly to the ground?" she gasped. "If those strings around my ankles break, it'll be goodbye for me!"

And that's what gave Mr Twit his second nasty idea.

Mrs Twit Goes Ballooning Up

"There's enough pull here to take me to the moon!" Mrs Twit cried out.

"To take you to *the moon*!" exclaimed Mr Twit. "What a ghastly thought! We wouldn't want anything like that to happen, oh dear me no!"

"We most certainly wouldn't!" cried Mrs Twit. "Put some more string around my ankles quickly! I want to feel absolutely safe!"

"Very well, my angel," said Mr Twit, and with a ghoulish grin on his lips he knelt down at her feet. He took a knife from his pocket and with one quick slash he cut through the strings holding Mrs Twit's ankles to the iron ring.

She went up like a rocket.

"Help!" she screamed. "Save me!"

But there was no saving her now. In a few seconds

she was high up in the blue blue sky and climbing fast.

Mr Twit stood below looking up. "*What* a pretty sight!" he said to himself. "How lovely all those balloons look in the sky! And what a marvellous bit of luck for me! At last the old hag is lost and gone for ever."

Mrs Twit Comes Ballooning Down

Mrs Twit may have been ugly and she may have been beastly, but she was not stupid.

High up there in the sky, she had a bright idea. "If I can get rid of some of these balloons," she said to herself, "I will stop going up and start to come down."

She began biting through the strings that held the balloons to her wrists and arms and neck and hair. Each time she bit through a string and let the balloon float away, the upward pull got less and her rate of climb slowed down.

When she had bitten through twenty strings, she stopped going up altogether. She stayed still in the air.

She bit through one more string.

Very very slowly, she began to float downwards.

It was a calm day. There was no wind at all. And because of this, Mrs Twit had gone absolutely straight up. She now began to come absolutely straight down.

As she floated gently down, Mrs Twit's petticoat

billowed out like a parachute, showing her long
knickers. It was a grand sight on a glorious day, and
thousands of birds came flying in from miles around to
stare at this extraordinary old woman in the sky.

Mr Twit Gets a Horrid Shock

Mr Twit, who thought he had seen his ugly wife for the last time, was sitting in the garden celebrating with a mug of beer.

Silently, Mrs Twit came floating down. When she was about the height of the house above Mr Twit, she suddenly called out at the top of her voice, "Here I come, you grizzly old grunion! You rotten old turnip! You filthy old frumpet!"

Mr Twit jumped as though he'd been stung by a giant wasp. He dropped his beer. He looked up. He gaped. He gasped. He gurgled. A few choking sounds came out of his mouth. "*Ughhhhhhhh!*" he said. "*Arghhhhhhhh! Ouchhhhhhhh!*"

"I'll get you for this!" shouted Mrs Twit. She was floating down right on top of him. She was purple with rage and slashing the air with her long walking-stick which she had somehow managed to hang on to all the time. "I'll swish you to a swazzle!" she shouted. "I'll swash you to a swizzle! I'll gnash you to a gnozzle! I'll gnosh you to a gnazzle!" And before Mr Twit had time to run away, this bundle of balloons and petticoats and fiery fury landed right on top of him, lashing out with the stick and cracking him all over his body.

The House, the Tree and the Monkey Cage

But that's enough of that. We can't go on for ever watching these two disgusting people doing disgusting things to each other. We must get ahead with the story.

Here is a picture of Mr and Mrs Twit's house and garden. Some house! It looks like a prison. And not a window anywhere.

"Who wants windows?" Mr Twit had said when they were building it. "Who wants every Tom, Dick and Harry peeping in to see what you're doing?" It didn't occur to Mr Twit that windows were meant mainly for looking out of, not for looking into.

And what do you think of that ghastly garden? Mrs Twit was the gardener. She was very good at growing thistles and stinging-nettles. "I always grow plenty of spiky thistles and plenty of stinging-nettles," she used to say. "They keep out nasty nosey little children."

Near the house you can see Mr Twit's workshed.

To one side there is The Big Dead Tree. It never has any leaves on it because it's dead.

And not far from the tree, you can see the monkey cage. There are four monkeys in it. They belong to Mr Twit. You will hear about them later.

Hugtight Sticky Glue

Once a week, on Wednesdays, the Twits had Bird Pie for supper. Mr Twit caught the birds and Mrs Twit cooked them.

Mr Twit was good at catching birds. On the day before Bird Pie day, he would put the ladder up against The Big Dead Tree and climb into the branches with a bucket of glue and a paint-brush. The glue he used was something called HUGTIGHT and it was stickier than any other glue in the world. He would paint it along the tops of all the branches and then go away.

As the sun went down, birds would fly in from all around to roost for the night in The Big Dead Tree. They didn't know, poor things, that the branches were all smeared with horrible HUGTIGHT. The moment they landed on a branch, their feet stuck and that was that.

The next morning, which was Bird Pie day, Mr Twit would climb up the ladder again and grab all the wretched birds that were stuck to the tree. It didn't matter what kind they were – song thrushes, blackbirds, sparrows, crows, little jenny wrens, robins, anything – they all went into the pot for Wednesday's Bird Pie supper.

Four Sticky Little Boys

On one Tuesday evening after Mr Twit had been up the ladder and smeared the tree with HUGTIGHT, four little boys crept into the garden to look at the monkeys. They didn't care about the thistles and stinging-nettles, not when there were monkeys to look at. After a while, they got tired of looking at the monkeys, so they explored further into the garden and found the ladder leaning against The Big Dead Tree. They decided to climb up it just for fun.

There's nothing wrong with that.

The next morning, when Mr Twit went out to collect the birds, he found four miserable little boys sitting in the tree, stuck as tight as could be by the seats of their pants to the branches. There were no birds because the presence of the boys had scared them away.

Mr Twit was furious. "As there are no birds for my pie tonight," he shouted, "then it'll have to be *boys* instead!" He started to climb the ladder. "Boys' Pie might be better than Birds' Pie," he went on, grinning horribly. "More meat and not so many tiny little bones!"

The boys were terrified. "He's going to boil us!" cried one of them.

"He'll stew us alive!" wailed the second one.

"He'll cook us with carrots!" cried the third.

But the fourth little boy, who had more sense than the others, whispered, "Listen, I've just had an idea.

We are only stuck by *the seats of our pants*. So quick! Unbutton your pants and slip out of them and fall to the ground."

Mr Twit had reached the top of the ladder and was just about to make a grab for the nearest boy when they all suddenly tumbled out of the tree and ran for home with their naked bottoms winking at the sun.

The Great Upside Down Monkey Circus

Now for the monkeys.

The four monkeys in the cage in the garden were all one family. They were Muggle-Wump and his wife and their two small children.

But what on earth were Mr and Mrs Twit doing with monkeys in their garden?

Well, in the old days, they had both worked in a circus as monkey trainers. They used to teach monkeys to do tricks and to dress up in human clothes and to smoke pipes and all the rest of that nonsense.

Today, although they were retired, Mr Twit still wanted to train monkeys. It was his dream that one day he would own the first GREAT UPSIDE DOWN MONKEY CIRCUS in the world.

That meant that the monkeys had to do everything upside down. They had to dance upside down (on their hands with their feet in the air). They had to play football upside down. They had to balance one on top of the other upside down, with Muggle-Wump at the bottom and the smallest baby monkey at the very top. They even had to eat and drink upside down and that is not an easy thing to do because the food and water has to go *up* your throat instead of down it. In fact, it is almost impossible, but the monkeys simply had to do it otherwise they got nothing.

All this sounds pretty silly to you and me. It sounded pretty silly to the monkeys, too. They absolutely hated having to do this upside down nonsense day after day. It made them giddy standing on their heads for hours on end. Sometimes the two small monkey children would faint with so much blood going to their heads. But Mr Twit didn't care about that. He kept them practising for six hours every day and if they didn't do as they were told, Mrs Twit would soon come running with her beastly stick.

The Roly-Poly Bird to the Rescue

Muggle-Wump and his family longed to escape from the cage in Mr Twit's garden and go back to the African jungle where they came from.

They hated Mr and Mrs Twit for making their lives so miserable.

They also hated them for what they did to the birds every Tuesday and Wednesday. "Fly away, birds!" they used to shout, jumping about in the cage and waving their arms. "Don't sit on that Big Dead Tree! It's just been smeared all over with sticky glue! Go and sit somewhere else!"

But these were English birds and they couldn't understand the weird African language the monkeys spoke. So they took no notice and went on using The Big Dead Tree and getting caught for Mrs Twit's Bird Pie.

Then one day, a truly magnificent bird flew down out of the sky and landed on the monkey cage.

"Good heavens!" cried all the monkeys together. "It's the Roly-Poly Bird! What on earth are you doing over here in England, Roly-Poly Bird?" Like the monkeys, the Roly-Poly Bird came from Africa and he spoke the same language as they did.

"I've come for a holiday," said the Roly-Poly Bird. "I like to travel." He fluffed his marvellous coloured feathers and looked down rather grandly at the monkeys. "For most people," he went on, "flying away on holiday is very expensive, but I can fly anywhere in the world for nothing."

"Do you know how to talk to these English birds?" Muggle-Wump asked him.

"Of course I do," said the Roly-Poly Bird. "'It's no good going to a country and not knowing the language."

"Then we must hurry," said Muggle-Wump. "Today is Tuesday and over there you can already see the revolting Mr Twit up the ladder painting sticky glue on all the branches of The Big Dead Tree. This evening when the birds come in to roost, you must warn them not to perch on that tree or they will be made into Bird Pie."

That evening, the Roly-Poly Bird flew round and round The Big Dead Tree singing out,

"There's sticky stick stuff all over the tree!
If you land in the branches, you'll never get free!
So fly away! Fly away! Stay up high!
Or you'll finish up tomorrow in a hot Bird Pie!"

No Bird Pie for Mr Twit

The next morning when Mr Twit came out with his huge basket to snatch all the birds from The Big Dead Tree, there wasn't a single one on it. They were all sitting on top of the monkey cage. The Roly-Poly Bird was there as well, and Muggle-Wump and his family were inside the cage and the whole lot of them were laughing at Mr Twit.

Still No Bird Pie for Mr Twit

Mr Twit wasn't going to wait another week for his Bird Pie supper. He loved Bird Pie. It was his favourite meal. So that very same day, he went after the birds again. This time he smeared all the top bars of the monkey cage with sticky glue, as well as the branches of the The Big Dead Tree. "Now I'll get you," he said, "whichever one you sit on!"

The monkeys crouched inside the cage watching all this, and later on, when the Roly-Poly Bird came swooping in for an evening chat, they shouted out,

"Don't land on our cage, Roly-Poly Bird! It's covered in sticky glue! So is the tree!"

And that evening, as the sun went down and all the birds came in again to roost, the Roly-Poly Bird flew round and round the monkey cage and The Big Dead Tree, singing out his warning,

"There's sticky stuff now on the cage *and* the tree!
If you land on either, you'll never get free!
So fly away! Fly away! Stay up high!
Or you'll finish up tomorrow in a hot Bird Pie!"

Mr and Mrs Twit Go Off to Buy Guns

The next morning when Mr Twit came out with his huge basket, not a single bird was sitting on either the monkey cage or The Big Dead Tree. They were all perched happily on the roof of Mr Twit's house. The Roly-Poly Bird was up there as well, and the monkeys were in the cage and the whole lot of them were hooting with laughter at Mr Twit.

"I'll wipe that silly laugh off your beaks!" Mr Twit screamed at the birds. "I'll get you next time, you filthy feathery frumps! I'll wring your necks, the whole lot of you, and have you bubbling in the pot for Bird Pie before this day is out!"

"How are you going to do that?" asked Mrs Twit, who had come outside to see what all the noise was about. "I won't have you smearing sticky glue all over the roof of our house!"

Mr Twit was very excited. "I've got a great idea!" he cried. He didn't bother to keep his voice down because he didn't think the monkeys could understand. "We'll both go into town right away and we'll buy a gun each!" he shouted. "How's that?"

"Brilliant!" cried Mrs Twit, grinning and showing her long yellow teeth. "We'll buy those big shotguns that spray out fifty bullets or more with each bang!"

"Exactly," said Mr Twit. "Lock up the house while I go and make sure the monkeys are safely shut away."

Mr Twit went over to the monkey cage. "Attention!" he barked in his fearsome monkey-trainer's voice. "Upside down all of you and jump to it! One on top of the other! Quick! Get on with it or you'll feel Mrs Twit's stick across your backsides!"

Obediently, the poor monkeys stood on their hands and clambered one on top of the other, with Muggle-Wump at the bottom and the smallest child at the very top.

"Now stay there till we come back!" Mr Twit ordered. "Don't you dare to move! And don't over-balance! When we return in two or three hours time, I shall expect to find you all in exactly the same position as you are now! You understand?"

With that, Mr Twit marched away. Mrs Twit went with him. And the monkeys were left alone with the birds.

Muggle-Wump Has an Idea

As soon as Mr and Mrs Twit had disappeared down the road, the monkeys all flipped back on to their feet the right way up. "Quick, get the key!" Muggle-Wump called out to the Roly-Poly Bird who was still sitting on the roof of the house.

"What key?" shouted the Roly-Poly Bird.

"The key to the door of our cage," cried Muggle-Wump. "It's hanging on a nail in the workshed. That's where he always puts it."

The Roly-Poly Bird flew down and came back with the key in his beak. Muggle-Wump reached a hand through the bars of the cage and took the key. He put it in the lock and turned it. The door opened. All four monkeys leapt out together.

"We are free!" cried the two little ones. "Where shall we go, Dad? Where shall we hide?"

"Don't get excited," said Muggle-Wump. "Calm down, everybody. Before we escape from this beastly place we have one very very important thing to do."

326

"What?" they asked him.

"We're going to turn those terrible Twits UPSIDE DOWN!"

"We're going to *what*?" they cried. "You must be joking, Dad!"

"I'm not joking," Muggle-Wump said. "We're going to turn both Mr and Mrs Twit UPSIDE DOWN with their legs in the air!"

"Don't be ridiculous," the Roly-Poly Bird said. "How can we possibly turn those two maggoty old monsters upside down?"

"We can, we can!" cried Muggle-Wump. "We are going to make them stand on their heads for hours and hours! Perhaps for ever! Let *them* see what it feels like for a change!"

"How?" said the Roly-Poly Bird. "Just tell me how."

Muggle-Wump laid his head on one side and a tiny twinkling little smile touched the corners of his mouth. "Now and again," he said, "but not very often, I have a brilliant idea. This is one of them. Follow me, my friends, follow me." He scampered off towards the house and the three other monkeys and the Roly-Poly Bird went after him.

"Buckets and paint-brushes!" cried Muggle-Wump. "That's what we want next! There are plenty in the workshed! Hurry up, everyone! Get a bucket and a paint-brush!"

Inside Mr Twit's workshed there was an enormous barrel of HUGTIGHT sticky glue, the stuff he used for catching birds. "Fill your buckets!" Muggle-Wump ordered. "We are now going into the big house!"

Mrs Twit had hidden the key to the front door under the mat and Muggle-Wump had seen her doing it, so it was easy for them to get in. In they went, all four monkeys, with their buckets of sticky glue. Then came the Roly-Poly Bird flying in after them, with a bucket in his beak and a brush in his claw.

The Great Glue Painting Begins

"This is the living-room," announced Muggle-Wump. "The grand and glorious living-room where those two fearful frumptious freaks eat Bird Pie every week for supper!"

"Please don't mention Bird Pie again," said the Roly-Poly Bird. "It gives me the shudders."

"We mustn't waste time!" cried Muggle-Wump. "Hurry up, hurry up! Now the first thing is this! I want everyone to paint sticky glue all over the ceiling! Cover it all! Smear it in every corner!"

"Over the ceiling!" they cried. "Why the *ceiling*?"

"Never mind why!" shouted Muggle-Wump. "Just do as you're told and don't argue!"

"But how do we get *up* there?" they asked. "We can't reach."

"Monkeys can reach anywhere!" shouted Muggle-Wump. He was in a frenzy of excitement now, waving his paint-brush and his bucket and leaping about all over the room. "Come on, come on! Jump on the table! Stand on the chairs! Hop on each other's shoulders! Roly-Poly can do it flying! Don't stand there gaping! We have to hurry, don't you understand that? Those terrible Twits will be back any moment and this time they'll have *guns*! Get on with it, for heaven's sake! Get on with it!"

And so the great glue-painting of the ceiling began. All the other birds who had been sitting on the roof flew in to help, carrying paint-brushes in their claws and beaks. There were buzzards, wild ducks, woodpeckers, magpies, rooks, ravens and many more. Everyone was splashing away like mad and with so many helpers, the job was soon finished.

The Carpet Goes on the Ceiling

"What now?" they all said, looking at Muggle-Wump.

"Ah-ha!" cried Muggle-Wump. "Now for the fun! Now for the greatest upside down trick of all time! Are you ready?"

"We're ready," said the monkeys. "We're ready," said the birds.

"Pull out the carpet!" shouted Muggle-Wump. "Pull this huge carpet out from under the furniture and stick it on to the ceiling!"

"On to the *ceiling*!" cried one of the small monkeys. "But that's impossible, Dad!"

"I'll stick *you* on to the ceiling if you don't shut up!" snapped Muggle-Wump.

"He's dotty!" they cried.

"He's balmy!"

"He's batty!"

"He's nutty!"

"He's screwy!"

"He's wacky!" cried the Roly-Poly Bird. "Poor old Muggles has gone off his wump at last!"

"Oh, do stop shouting such rubbish and give me a hand," said Muggle-Wump, catching hold of one corner of the carpet. "Pull, you nitwits, pull!"

The carpet was enormous. It covered the entire floor from wall to wall. It had a red and gold pattern on it. It is not easy to pull an enormous carpet off the floor when the room is full of tables and chairs. "Pull!" yelled Muggle-Wump. "Pull, pull, pull!" He was like a demon hopping round the room and telling everyone what to do. But you couldn't blame him. After months and months of standing on his head with his family, he couldn't wait for the time when the terrible Twits would be doing the same thing. At least that's what he hoped.

With the monkeys and the birds all pulling and puffing, the carpet was dragged off the floor and finally hoisted up on to the ceiling. And there it stuck.

All at once, the whole ceiling of the living-room was carpeted in red and gold.

The Furniture Goes Up

"Now the table, the big table!" shouted Muggle-Wump. "Turn the table upside down and put a dollop of sticky glue on to the bottom of each leg. Then we shall stick that on to the ceiling as well!"

Hoisting the huge table upside down on to the ceiling was not an easy job, but they managed it in the end.

"Will it stay there?" they cried. "Is the glue strong enough to hold it up?"

"It's the strongest glue in the world!" Muggle-Wump replied. "It's the special bird-catching bird-killing glue for smearing on trees!"

"Please," said the Roly-Poly Bird. "I have asked you before not to mention that subject. How would *you* like it if it was Monkey Pie they made every

Wednesday and all your friends had been boiled up and I went on talking about it?"

"I do beg your pardon," said Muggle-Wump. "I'm so excited I hardly know what I'm saying. Now the chairs! Do the same with the chairs! All the chairs must be stuck upside down to the ceiling! And in their right places! Oh, do hurry up, everybody! Any moment now, those two filthy freaks are going to come rushing in with their guns!"

The monkeys, with the birds helping them, put glue on the bottom of each chair leg and hoisted them up to the ceiling.

"Now the smaller tables!" shouted Muggle-Wump. "And the big sofa! And the sideboard! And the lamps! And all the tiny little things! The ashtrays! The ornaments! And that beastly plastic gnome on the sideboard! Everything, absolutely everything must be stuck to the ceiling!"

It was terribly hard work. It was especially difficult to stick everything on to the ceiling in exactly its right place. But they got it done in the end.

"What now?" asked the Roly-Poly Bird. He was out of breath and so tired he could hardly flap his wings.

"Now the pictures!" cried Muggle-Wump. "Turn all the pictures upside down! And will one of you birds please fly out on to the road and watch to see when those frumptious freaks are coming back."

"I'll go," said the Roly-Poly Bird. "I'll sit on the telephone wires and keep guard. It'll give me a rest."

The Ravens Swoop Over

They had only just finished the job when the Roly-Poly Bird came swooping in, screaming, "They're coming back! They're coming back!"

Quickly, the birds flew back on to the roof of the house. The monkeys rushed into their cage and stood upside down one on top of the other. A moment later, Mr and Mrs Twit came marching into the garden, each carrying a fearsome-looking gun.

"I'm glad to see those monkeys are still upside down," said Mr Twit.

"They're too stupid to do anything else," said Mrs Twit. "Hey, look at all those cheeky birds still up there on the roof! Let's go inside and load our lovely new guns and then it'll be *bang bang bang* and Bird Pie for supper."

Just as Mr and Mrs Twit were about to enter the house, two black ravens swooped low over their heads. Each bird carried a paint-brush in its claw and each paint-brush was smeared with sticky glue. As the ravens whizzed over, they brushed a streak of sticky glue on to the tops of Mr and Mrs Twit's heads. They did it with the lightest touch but even so the Twits both felt it.

"What was *that*?" cried Mrs Twit. "Some beastly bird has dropped his dirty droppings on my head!"

"On mine too!" shouted Mr Twit. "I felt it! I felt it!"

"Don't touch it!" cried Mrs Twit. "You'll get it all over your hands! Come inside and we'll wash it off at the sink!"

"The filthy dirty brutes," yelled Mr Twit. "I'll bet they did it on purpose! Just wait till I've loaded up my gun!"

Mrs Twit got the key from under the doormat (where Muggle-Wump had carefully replaced it) and into the house they went.

The Twits Are Turned Upside Down

"*What's this?*" gasped Mr Twit as they entered the living-room.

"*What's happened?*" screamed Mrs Twit.

They stood in the middle of the room, looking up.

All the furniture, the big table, the chairs, the sofa, the lamps, the little side tables, the cabinet with bottles of beer in it, the ornaments, the electric fire, the carpet, everything was stuck upside down to the ceiling. The pictures were upside down on the walls. And the floor they were standing on was absolutely bare. What's more, it had been painted white to look like the ceiling.

"*Look!*" screamed Mrs Twit. "*That's the floor! The floor's up there! This is the ceiling! We are standing on the ceiling!*"

"We're UPSIDE DOWN!" gasped Mr Twit. "We *must* be upside down. We are standing on the ceiling looking down at the floor!"

"Oh help!" screamed Mrs Twit. "Help help help! I'm beginning to feel giddy!"

"So am I! So am I!" cried Mr Twit. "I don't like this one little bit!"

"We're upside down and all the blood's going to my head!" screamed Mrs Twit. "If we don't do something quickly, I shall die, I know I will!"

"I've got it!" cried Mr Twit. "I know what we'll do!

346

We'll stand on our heads, then anyway we'll be the right way up!"

So they stood on their heads, and of course, the moment the tops of their heads touched the floor, the sticky glue that the ravens had brushed on a few moments before did its job. They were stuck. They were pinned down, cemented, glued, fixed to the floorboards.

Through a crack in the door the monkeys watched. They'd jumped right out of their cage the moment the Twits had gone inside. And the Roly-Poly Bird watched. And all the other birds flew in and out to catch a glimpse of this extraordinary sight.

The Monkeys Escape

That evening, Muggle-Wump and his family went up to the big wood on top of the hill, and in the tallest tree of all they built a marvellous tree-house. All the birds, especially the big ones, the crows and rooks and magpies, made their nests around the tree-house so that nobody could see it from the ground.

"You can't stay up here for ever, you know," the Roly-Poly Bird said.

"Why not?" asked Muggle-Wump. "It's a lovely place."

"Just you wait till the winter comes," the Roly-Poly Bird said. "Monkeys don't like cold weather, do they?"

"They most certainly don't!" cried Muggle-Wump. "Are the winters so very cold over here?"

"It's all snow and ice," said the Roly-Poly Bird. "Sometimes it's so cold a bird will wake up in the morning with his feet frozen to the bough that he's been roosting on."

"Then what shall we do?" cried Muggle-Wump. "My family will all be deep-freezed!"

"No, they won't," said the Roly-Poly Bird. "Because when the first leaves start falling from the trees in the autumn, you can all fly home to Africa with me."

"Don't be ridiculous," Muggle-Wump said. "Monkeys can't fly."

"You can sit on my back," said the Roly-Poly Bird. "I shall take you one at a time. You will travel by the Roly-Poly Super Jet and it won't cost you a penny!"

The Twits Get the Shrinks

And down here in the horrid house, Mr and Mrs Twit are still stuck upside down to the floor of the living-room.

"It's all your fault!" yelled Mr Twit, thrashing his legs in the air. "*You're* the one, you ugly old cow, who went hopping around shouting 'We're upside down! We're upside down!' "

"And *you're* the one who said to stand on our heads so we'd be the right way up, you whiskery old warthog!" screamed Mrs Twit. "Now we'll never get free! We're stuck here for ever!"

"*You* may be stuck here for ever," said Mr Twit. "But not me! I'm going to get away!"

Mr Twit wriggled and squirmed, and he squiggled and wormed, and he twisted and turned, and he choggled and churned, but the sticky glue held him to the floor just as tightly as it had once held the poor birds in The Big Dead Tree. He was still as upside down as ever, standing on his head.

But heads are not made to be stood upon. If you stand on your head for a very long time, a horrid thing happens, and this was where Mr Twit got his biggest shock of all. With so much weight on it from up above, his head began to get squashed into his body.

Quite soon, it had disappeared completely, sunk out of sight in the fatty folds of his flabby neck.

"I'm SHRINKING!" burbled Mr Twit.

"So am I!" cried Mrs Twit.

"Help me! Save me! Call a doctor!" yelled Mr Twit. "I'm getting THE DREADED SHRINKS!"

And so he was. Mrs Twit was getting THE DREADED SHRINKS, too! And this time it wasn't a fake. It was the real thing!

Their heads SHRANK into their necks . . .

Then their necks began SHRINKING into their bodies . . .

And their bodies began SHRINKING into their legs . . .

And their legs began SHRINKING into their feet . . .

And one week later, on a nice sunny afternoon, a man called Fred came round to read the gas meter. When nobody answered the door, Fred peeped into the house and there he saw, on the floor of the living-room, two bundles of old clothes, two pairs of shoes and a walking-stick. There was nothing more left in this world of Mr and Mrs Twit.

And everyone, including Fred, shouted ... "HOORAY!"

Roald Dahl

The Giraffe and the Pelly and Me

Illustrated by Quentin Blake

For Neisha, Charlotte and Lorina

Nᴏᴛ ꜰᴀʀ from where I live there is a queer old empty wooden house standing all by itself on the side of the road. I long to explore inside it but the door is always locked, and when I peer through a window all I can see is darkness and dust. I know the ground floor used once to be a shop because I can still read the faded lettering across the front which says ᴛʜᴇ ɢʀᴜʙʙᴇʀ. My mother has told me that in our part of the country in the olden days a grubber was another name for a sweet-shop, and now every time I look at it I think to myself what a lovely old sweet-shop it must have been.

On the shop-window itself somebody has painted in white the words ꜰᴏʀ ꜱᴀɪʟ.

One morning, I noticed that ꜰᴏʀ ꜱᴀɪʟ had been scraped off the shop-window and in its place somebody had painted ꜱᴏʟᴇᴅ. I stood there staring at the new writing and wishing like mad that it had been me who had bought it because then I would have been able to make it into a grubber all over again. I have always longed and longed to own a sweet-shop. The sweet-shop of my dreams would be loaded from top to bottom with Sherbet Suckers and Caramel Fudge and

Russian Toffee and Sugar Snorters and Butter Gumballs and thousands and thousands of other glorious things like that. Oh boy, what I couldn't have done with that old Grubber shop if it had been mine!

On my next visit to The Grubber, I was standing across the road gazing at the wonderful old building when suddenly an enormous bathtub came sailing out through one of the second-floor windows and crashed right on to the middle of the road!

A few moments later, a white porcelain lavatory pan with the wooden seat still on it came flying out of the same window and landed with a wonderful splintering crash just beside the bathtub. This was followed by a kitchen sink and an empty canary-cage and a four-poster bed and two hot-water bottles and a rocking horse and a sewing-machine and goodness knows what else besides.

It looked as though some madman was ripping out the whole of the inside of the house, because now pieces of staircase and bits of the banisters and a whole lot of old floorboards came whistling through the windows.

Then there was silence. I waited and waited but not another sound came from within the building. I crossed the road and stood right under the windows and called out, "Is anybody at home?"

There was no answer.

In the end it began to get dark so I had to turn away and start walking home. But you can bet your life nothing was going to stop me from hurrying back there again tomorrow morning to see what the next surprise was going to be.

When I got back to the Grubber house the next morning, the first thing I noticed was the new door. The dirty old brown door had been taken out and in its place someone had fitted a brand-new red one. The new door was fantastic. It was twice as high as the other one had been and it looked ridiculous. I couldn't begin to imagine who would want a tremendous tall door like that in his house unless it was a giant.

As well as this, somebody had scraped away the SOLED notice on the shop-window and now there was a whole lot of different writing all over the glass. I stood there reading it and reading it and trying to figure out what on earth it all meant.

The LWC Co

THE LADDERLESS
WINDOW·CLEANING
COMPANY ~
Get your windows
cleaned without
a lot of dirty
ladders leaning
against your
house.

I tried to catch some sign or sound of movement inside the house but there was none . . . until all of a sudden . . . out of the corner of my eye . . . I noticed that one of the windows on the top floor was slowly beginning to open outwards . . .

Then a HEAD appeared at the open window.

I stared at the head. The head stared back at me with big round dark eyes.

Suddenly, a second window was flung wide open and of all the crazy things a gigantic white bird hopped out and perched on the window-sill. I knew what this

one was because of its amazing beak which was shaped like a huge orange-coloured basin. The Pelican looked down at me and sang out:

> *"Oh, how I wish*
> *For a big fat fish!*
> *I'm as hungry as ever could be!*
> *A dish of fish is my only wish!*
> *How far are we from the sea?"*

"We are a long way from the sea," I called back to him, "but there is a fishmonger in the village not far away."

"A fish *what*?"

"A fish*monger*."

"Now what on earth would that be?" asked the Pelican. "I have heard of a fish-*pie* and a fish-*cake* and a fish-*finger*, but I have never heard of a fish-*monger*. Are these mongers good to eat?"

This question baffled me a bit, so I said, "Who is your friend in the next window?"

"She is the Giraffe!" the Pelican answered. "Is she not wonderful? Her legs are on the ground floor and her head is looking out of the top window!"

As if all this wasn't enough, the window on the *first floor* was now flung wide open and out popped a Monkey!

The Monkey stood on the window-sill and did a jiggly little dance. He was so skinny he seemed to be made only out of furry bits of wire, but he danced wonderfully well, and I clapped and cheered and did a little dance myself in return.

THE LADYKILLERS
WINDOW-CLEANING
COMPANY ~

Get your windows
cleaned within
a lot of dirty
Ladders leaning
against your
house.

"We are the Window-Cleaners!" sang out the Monkey.

"We will polish your glass
Till it's shining like brass
And it sparkles like sun on the sea!
We are quick and polite,
We will come day or night,
The Giraffe and the Pelly and me!

We're a fabulous crew,
We know just what to do,
And we never stop work to drink tea.
All your windows will glow
When we give them a go,
The Giraffe and the Pelly and me!

We use water and soap
Plus some kindness and hope,
But we never use ladders, not we.
Who needs ladders at all
When you're thirty feet tall?
Not Giraffe, and not Pelly! Not me!"

I stood there enthralled. Then I heard the Giraffe saying to the Pelican in the next window, "Pelly, my dear, be so good as to fly down and bring that small person up here to talk to us."

At once the Pelican spread his huge white wings and flew down on to the road beside me. "Hop in," he said, opening his enormous beak.

I stared at the great orange beak and backed away.

"Go ON!" the Monkey shouted from up in his window. "The Pelly isn't going to *swallow* you! Climb IN!"

I said to the Pelican, "I'll only get in if you promise not to shut your beak once I'm inside."

"You have nothing to fear!" cried the Pelican,

"And let me tell you why.
I have a very special beak!
A special beak have I!
You'll never see a beak so fine,
I don't care where you go.
There's magic in this beak of mine!
Hop in and don't say NO!"

"I will *not* hop in," I said, "unless you swear on your honour you won't shut it once I'm inside. I don't like small dark places."

"When I have done what I am just about to do," said the Pelican, "I won't be *able* to shut it. You don't seem to understand how my beak works."

"Show me," I said.

"Watch this!" cried the Pelican.

I watched in amazement as the top half of the Pelican's beak began to slide smoothly backwards into his head until the whole thing was almost out of sight.

"It bends and goes down inside the back of my neck!" cried the Pelican. "Is that not sensible? Is it not magical?"

"It's unbelievable," I said. "It's exactly like one of those metal tape-measures my father's got at home. When it's out, it's straight. When you slide it back in, it bends and disappears."

"Precisely," said the Pelican. "You see, the top half is of no use to me unless I am chewing fish. The bottom half is what counts, my lad! The bottom half of this glorious beak of mine is the bucket in which we carry our window-cleaning water! So if I didn't slide the top half away I'd be standing around all day long holding it open!

> *"So I slide it away*
> *For the rest of the day!*
> *Even so, I'm still able to speak!*
> *And wherever I've flown*
> *It has always been known*
> *As the Pelican's Patented Beak!*

If I want to eat fish
(That's my favourite dish)
All I do is I give it a tweak!
In the blink of an eye
Out it pops! And they cry,
'It's the Pelican's Patented Beak!'"

"Stop showing off down there!" shouted the Monkey from the upstairs window. "Hurry up and bring that small person up to us! The Giraffe is waiting!"

I climbed into the big orange beak, and with a swoosh of wings the Pelican carried me back to his perch on the window-sill.

The Giraffe looked out of her window at me and said, "How do you do? What is your name?"

"Billy," I told her.

"Well, Billy," she said, "we need your help and we need it fast. We *must have* some windows to clean. We've spent every penny we had on buying this house and we've got to earn some more money quickly. The Pelly is starving, the Monkey is famished and I am perishing with hunger. The Pelly needs fish. The Monkey needs nuts and I am even more difficult to feed. I am a Geraneous Giraffe and a Geraneous Giraffe cannot eat anything except the pink and purple flowers of the tinkle-tinkle tree. But those, as I am sure you know, are hard to find and expensive to buy."

The Pelican cried out, "Right now I am so hungry I could eat a stale sardine!

> *"Has anyone seen a stale sardine*
> *Or a bucket of rotten cod?*
> *I'd eat the lot upon the spot,*
> *I'm such a hungry bod!"*

Every time the Pelican spoke, the beak I was standing in jiggled madly up and down, and the more excited he got, the more it jiggled.

The Monkey said, "What Pelly's *really* crazy about is salmon!"

"Yes, yes!" cried the Pelican. "Salmon! Oh, glorious salmon! I dream about it all day long but I never get any!"

"And *I* dream about walnuts!" shouted the Monkey. "A walnut fresh from the tree is scrumptious-galumptious, so flavory-savory, so sweet to eat that it makes me all wobbly just thinking about it!"

At exactly that moment, a huge white Rolls-Royce pulled up right below us, and a chauffeur in a blue and gold uniform got out. He was carrying an envelope in one gloved hand.

"Good heavens!" I whispered. "That's the Duke of Hampshire's car!"

"Who's he?" asked the Giraffe.

"He's the richest man in England!" I said.

The chauffeur knocked on the door of The Grubber.

He looked up and saw us. He saw the Giraffe, the
Pelly, the Monkey and me all staring down at him
from above, but not a muscle moved in his face, not an
eyebrow was raised. The chauffeurs of very rich men
are never surprised by anything they see. The chauffeur said, "His Grace The Duke of Hampshire has
instructed me to deliver this envelope to The Ladderless Window-Cleaning Company."

"That's us!" cried the Monkey.

The Giraffe said, "Be so good as to open the
envelope and read us the letter."

The chauffeur unfolded the letter and began to read, "'Dear Sirs, I saw your notice as I drove by this morning. I have been looking for a decent window-cleaner for the last fifty years but I have not found one yet. My house has six hundred and seventy-seven windows in it (not counting the greenhouse) and all of them are filthy. Kindly come and see me as soon as possible. Yours truly, Hampshire.' That", added the chauffeur in a voice filled with awe and respect, "was written by His Grace The Duke of Hampshire in his own hand."

The Giraffe said to the chauffeur, "Please tell His Grace The Duke that we will be with him as soon as possible."

The chauffeur touched his cap and got back into the Rolls-Royce.

"Whoopee!" shouted the Monkey.

"Fantastic!" cried the Pelican. "That must be the best window-cleaning job in the world!"

"Billy," said the Giraffe, "what is the house called and how do we get there?"

"It is called Hampshire House," I said. "It's just over the hill. I'll show you the way."

"We're off!" cried the Monkey. "We're off to see the Duke!"

The Giraffe stooped low and went out through the tall door. The Monkey jumped off the window-sill on to the Giraffe's back. The Pelican, with me in his beak hanging on for dear life, flew across and perched on the very top of the Giraffe's head. And away we went.

It wasn't long before we came to the gates of Hampshire House, and as the Giraffe moved slowly up the great wide driveway, we all began to feel just a little bit nervous.

"What's he like, this Duke?" the Giraffe asked me.

"I don't know," I said. "But he's very very famous and very rich. People say he has twenty-five gardeners just to look after his flower-beds."

Soon the huge house itself came into view, and what a house it was! It was like a palace! It was bigger than a palace!

"Just look at those windows!" cried the Monkey. "They'll keep us going for ever!"

Then suddenly we heard a man's voice a short distance away to the right. "I want those big black ones at the top of the tree!" the man was shouting. "Get me those great big black ones!"

We peered round the bushes and saw an oldish man with an immense white moustache standing under a tall cherry tree and pointing his walking-stick in the air. There was a ladder against the tree and another man, who was probably a gardener, was up the ladder.

"Get me those great big black juicy ones right at the very top!" the old man was shouting.

"I can't reach them, Your Grace," the gardener called back. "The ladder isn't long enough!"

"Damnation!" shouted the Duke. "I *was* so looking forward to eating those big ones!"

"Here we go!" the Pelican whispered to me, and
with a swish and a swoop he carried me up to the very
top of the cherry tree and there he perched. "Pick
them, Billy!" he whispered. "Pick them quickly and
put them in my beak!"

The gardener got such a shock he fell off the ladder.
Down below us, the Duke was shouting, "My gun!
Get me my gun! Some damnable monster of a bird is
stealing my best cherries! Be off with you, sir! Go
away! Those are *my* cherries, not yours! I'll have you
shot for this, sir! Where *is* my gun?"

"Hurry, Billy!" whispered the Pelican. "Hurry,
hurry, hurry!"

"My gun!" the Duke was shouting to the gardener.
"Get me my gun, you idiot! I'll have that thieving bird
for breakfast, you see if I don't."

"I've picked them all," I whispered to the Pelican.

At once the Pelly flew down and landed right beside the furious figure of the Duke of Hampshire, who was prancing about and waving his stick in the air!

"Your cherries, Your Grace!" I said as I leaned over the edge of the Pelican's beak and offered a handful to the Duke.

The Duke was staggered. He reeled back and his eyes popped nearly out of their sockets. "Great Scott!" he gasped. "Good Lord! What's this? Who are *you*?"

And now the Giraffe, with the Monkey dancing about on her back, emerged suddenly from the bushes. The Duke stared at them. He looked as though he was about to have a fit.

"*Who are these creatures?*" he bellowed. "Has the whole world gone completely dotty?"

"We are the window-cleaners!" sang out the Monkey.

> "*We will polish your glass*
> *Till it's shining like brass*
> *And it sparkles like sun on the sea!*
> *We will work for Your Grace*
> *Till we're blue in the face,*
> *The Giraffe and the Pelly and me!*"

"You *asked* us to come and see you," the Giraffe said.

The truth was at last beginning to dawn on the
Duke. He put a cherry into his mouth and chewed it
slowly. Then he spat out the stone. "I like the way you
picked these cherries for me," he said. "Could you also
pick my apples in the autumn?"

"We could! We could! Of course we could!" we all
shouted.

"And who are *you*?" the Duke said, pointing his
stick at me.

"He is our Business Manager," the Giraffe said.
"His name is Billy. We go nowhere without him."

"Very well, very well," the Duke muttered. "Come
along with me and let's see if you're any good at clean-
ing windows."

I climbed out of the Pelican's beak and the kindly old Duke took me by the hand as we all walked towards the house. When we got there, the Duke said, "What happens next?"

"It is all very simple, Your Grace," the Giraffe replied. "I am the ladder, the Pelly is the bucket and the Monkey is the cleaner. Watch us go!"

With that, the famous window-cleaning gang sprang into action. The Monkey jumped down from the Giraffe's back and turned on the garden tap. The Pelican held his great beak under the tap until it was full of water. Then, with a wonderful springy leap the Monkey leaped up once again on to the Giraffe's back.

From there he scrambled, as easily as if he were climbing a tree, up the long long neck of the Giraffe until he stood balancing on the very top of her head. The Pelican remained standing on the ground beside us, looking up at the Giraffe.

"We'll do the top floor first!" the Giraffe shouted down. "Bring the water up, please."

The Duke called out, "Don't worry about the two top floors. You can't reach them anyway."

"Who says we can't reach them?" the Giraffe called back.

"I do," the Duke said firmly, "And I'm not having any of you risking your silly necks around here."

If you wish to be friends with a Giraffe, never say anything bad about its neck. Its neck is its proudest possession.

"What's wrong with my neck?" snapped the Giraffe.

"Don't argue with me, you foolish creature!" cried the Duke. "If you can't reach it, you can't reach it and that's the end of it! Now get on with your work!"

"Your Grace," the Giraffe said, giving the Duke a small superior smile, "there are no windows in the world I cannot reach with this magical neck of mine."

The Monkey, who was dancing about most dangerously on top of the Giraffe's head, cried out, "Show him, Giraffey! Go on and show him what you can do with your magical neck!"

The next moment, the Giraffe's neck, which heaven knows was long enough already, began to grow longer
and L O N G E R

and L O N G E R

and L O N G E R

and HIGHER

and HIGHER

and HIGHER

until at last the Giraffe's head with the Monkey on top
of it was level with the windows of the top floor.

The Giraffe looked down from her great height and
said to the Duke, "How's that?"

The Duke was speechless. So was I. It was the most
magical thing I had ever seen, more magical even than
the Pelican's Patented Beak.

Up above us, the Giraffe was beginning to sing a little song, but she sang so softly I could hardly catch the words. I think it went something like this:

"My neck can stretch terribly high,
Much higher than eagles can fly.
If I ventured to show
Just how high it would go
You'd lose sight of my head in the sky!"

The Pelican, with his huge beak full of water, flew up and perched on one of the top-floor window-sills near the Monkey, and now the great window-cleaning business really began.

The speed with which the team worked was astonishing. As soon as one window was done, the Giraffe moved the Monkey over to the next one and the Pelican followed.

When all the fourth-floor windows on that side of the house were finished, the Giraffe simply drew in her magical neck until the Monkey was level with the third-floor windows and off they went again.

"Amazing!" cried the Duke. "Astonishing! Remarkable! Incredible! I haven't seen out of any of my windows for forty years! Now I shall be able to sit indoors and enjoy the view!"

Suddenly I saw all three of the Window-Cleaners stop dead in their tracks. They seemed to freeze against the wall of the house. None of them moved.

"What's happened to them?" the Duke asked me. "What's gone wrong?"

"I don't know," I answered.

Then the Giraffe, with the Monkey on her head, tiptoed very gingerly away from the house and came towards us. The Pelican flew with them. The Giraffe came up very close to the Duke and whispered, "Your Grace, there is a man in one of the bedrooms on the third floor. He is opening all the drawers and taking things out. He's got a pistol!"

The Duke jumped about a foot in the air. "Which room?" he snapped. "Show me at once!"

"It's the one on the third floor where the window is wide open," the Giraffe whispered.

"By Gad!" cried the Duke. "That's the Duchess's bedroom! He's after her jewels! Call the police! Summon the army! Bring up the cannon! Charge with the Light Brigade!" But even as he spoke the Pelican was flying up into the air. As he flew, he turned himself upside-down and tipped the window-cleaning water out of his beak. Then I saw the top half of that marvellous patented beak sliding out of his head, ready for action.

"What's that crazy bird up to?" cried the Duke.

"Wait and see," shouted the Monkey. "Hold your breath, old man! Hold your nose! Hold your horses and watch the Pelly go!"

Like a bullet the Pelican flew in through the open-window, and five seconds later out he came again with his great orange beak firmly closed. He landed on the lawn beside the Duke.

A tremendous banging noise was coming from inside the Pelican's beak. It sounded as though some-one was using a sledgehammer against it from the inside.

"He's got him!" cried the Monkey. "Pelly's got the burglar in his beak!"

"Well done, sir!" shouted the Duke, hopping about with excitement. Suddenly he pulled the handle of his walking-stick upwards, and out of the hollow inside of the stick itself he drew a long thin sharp shining sword. "I'll run him through!" he shouted, flourishing the sword like a fencer. "Open up, Pelican! Let me get at him! I'll run the bounder through before he knows what's happened to him! I'll spike him like a pat of butter! I'll feed his gizzards to my foxhounds!"

But the Pelican did not open his beak. He kept it firmly closed and shook his head at the Duke.

The Giraffe shouted, "The burglar is armed with a pistol, Your Grace! If Pelly lets him out now he'll shoot us all!"

"He can be armed with a *machine-gun* for all I care!" bellowed the Duke, his massive moustaches bristling like brushwood. "I'll handle the blighter! Open up, sir! Open up!"

Suddenly there was an ear-splitting BANG and the Pelican leaped twenty feet into the air. So did the Duke.

"Watch out!" the Duke shouted, taking ten rapid paces backwards. "He's trying to shoot his way out!" And pointing his sword at the Pelican, he bellowed, "Keep that beak closed, sir! Don't you dare let him out! He'll murder us all!"

"Shake him up, Pelly!" cried the Giraffe. "Rattle his bones! Teach him not to do it again!"

The Pelican shook his head so fast from side to side that the beak became a blur and the man inside must have felt he was being scrambled like eggs.

"Well done, Pelly!" cried the Giraffe. "You're doing a great job! Keep on shaking him so he doesn't fire that pistol again!"

At this point, a lady with an enormous chest and flaming orange hair came flying out of the house screaming, "My jewels! Somebody's stolen my jewels! My diamond tiara! My diamond necklace! My diamond bracelets! My diamond earrings! My diamond rings! They've had the lot! My rooms have been ransacked!"

And then this massive female, who fifty-five years ago had been a world-famous opera-singer, suddenly burst into song.

"My diamonds are over the ocean,
My diamonds are over the sea,
My diamonds were pinched from my bedroom,
Oh, bring back my diamonds to me."

We were so bowled over by the power of the lady's lungs that all of us, excepting the Pelican, who had to keep his beak closed, joined in the chorus.

"Bring back, bring back,
Oh, bring back my diamonds to me, to me.
Bring back, bring back,
Oh, bring back my diamonds to me!"

"Calm yourself, Henrietta," said the Duke. He
pointed to the Pelican and said, "This clever bird, this
brilliant burglar-catching creature has saved the day!
The bounder's in his beak!"

The Duchess stared at the Pelican. The Pelican
stared back at the Duchess and gave her a wink.

"If he's in there," cried the Duchess, "why don't
you let him out! Then you can run him through with
that famous sword of yours! I want my diamonds!
Open your beak, bird!"

"No, no!" shouted the Duke. "He's got a pistol!
He'll murder us all!"

Someone must have called the police because suddenly no less than four squad cars came racing towards
us with their sirens screaming.

Within seconds we were surrounded by six policemen, and the Duke was shouting to them, "The villain

you are after is inside the beak of that bird! Stand by
to collar him!" And to the Pelican he said, "Get ready
to open up! Are you ready ... steady ... *go*! Open her
up!"

The Pelican opened his gigantic beak and
immediately the policemen pounced upon the burglar
who was crouching inside. They snatched his pistol
away from him and dragged him out and put hand-
cuffs on his wrists.

"Great Scott!" shouted the Chief of Police. "It's the
Cobra himself!"

"The who! The what!" everyone asked. "Who's the
Cobra?"

"The Cobra is the cleverest and most dangerous cat-
burglar in the world!" said the Chief of Police. "He
must have climbed up the drainpipe. The Cobra can
climb up anything!"

"My diamonds!" screamed the Duchess. "I want my diamonds! Where are my diamonds?"

"Here they are!" cried the Chief of Police, fishing great handfuls of jewellery from the burglar's pockets.

The Duchess was so overcome with relief that she fell to the ground in a faint.

When the police had taken away the fearsome burglar known as the Cobra, and the fainting Duchess had been carried into the house by her servants, the old Duke stood on the lawn with the Giraffe, the Pelican, the Monkey and me.

"Look!" cried the Monkey. "That rotten burglar's bullet has made a hole in poor Pelly's beak!"

"That's done it," said the Pelican. "Now it won't be any use for holding water when we clean the windows."

"Don't you worry about that, my dear Pelly," said the Duke, patting him on the beak. "My chauffeur will soon put a patch over it the same way he mends the tyres on the Rolls. Right now we have far more important things to talk about than a little hole in a beak."

We stood there waiting to see what the Duke was going to say next.

"Now listen to me, all of you," he said. "Those diamonds were worth millions! Millions and millions! and *you* have saved them!"

The Monkey nodded. The Giraffe smiled. The Pelican blushed.

"No reward is too great for you," the Duke went on. "I am therefore going to make you an offer which I hope will give you pleasure. I hereby invite the Giraffe and the Pelican and the Monkey to live on my estate for the rest of their lives.

"I shall give you my best and largest hay-barn as your private house. Central heating, showers, a kitchen and anything else you desire for your comfort will be installed.

"In return, you will keep my windows clean, and pick my cherries and my apples. If the Pelican is willing, perhaps he will also give me a ride in his beak now and again."

"A pleasure, Your Grace!" cried the Pelican. "Would you like a ride now?"

"Later," said the Duke. "I'll have one after tea."

At this point, the Giraffe gave a nervous little cough and looked up at the sky.

"Is there a problem?" asked the Duke. "If there is, do please let me hear it."

"I don't like to sound ungrateful or pushy," murmured the Giraffe, "but we do have one very pressing problem. We are all absolutely famished. We haven't eaten for days."

"My *dear* Giraffey!" cried the Duke. "How very thoughtless of me. Food is no problem around here."

"I'm afraid it is not quite as easy as all that," said the Giraffe. "You see, I myself happen to be ..."

"Don't tell me!" cried the Duke. "I know it already! I am an expert on the animals of Africa. The moment I saw you I knew you were no ordinary giraffe. You are of the Geraneous variety, are you not?"

"You are absolutely right, Your Grace," said the Giraffe. "But the trouble with us is that we only eat ..."

"You don't have to tell me that either!" cried the Duke. "I know perfectly well a Geraneous Giraffe can eat only one kind of food. Am I not right in thinking that the pink and purple flowers of the tinkle-tinkle tree are your only diet?"

"Yes," sighed the Giraffe, "and that's been my problem ever since I arrived on these shores."

"That is no problem at all here at Hampshire House," said the Duke. "Look over there, my dear Giraffey, and you will see the only plantation of tinkle-tinkle trees in the entire country!"

The Giraffe looked. She gave a gasp of astonishment, and at first she was so overwhelmed she couldn't even speak. Great tears of joy began running down her cheeks.

"Help yourself," said the Duke. "Eat all you want."

"Oh, my sainted souls!" gasped the Giraffe. "Oh, my naked neck! I cannot *believe* what I am seeing!"

The next moment she was galloping full speed across the lawns and whinnying with excitement and the last we saw of her, she was burying her head in the beautiful pink and purple flowers that blossomed on the tops of the trees all around her.

"As for the Monkey," the Duke went on, "I think he also will be pleased with what I have to offer. All over my estate there are thousands of giant nut trees ..."

"Nuts?" cried the Monkey. "What kind of nuts?"

"Walnuts, of course," said the Duke.

"*Walnuts!*" screamed the Monkey. "Not *walnuts*? You don't really mean *walnuts*? You're pulling my leg! You're joking! You can't be serious! I must have heard wrong!"

"There's a walnut tree right over there," the Duke said, pointing.

The Monkey took off like an arrow, and a few seconds later he was high up in the branches of the walnut tree, cracking the nuts and guzzling what was inside.

"That leaves only the Pelly," said the Duke.

"Yes," said the Pelican nervously, "but I'm afraid that what I eat does not grow on trees. I only eat fish. Would it be too much trouble, I wonder, if I were to ask you for a reasonably fresh piece of haddock or cod every day?"

"Haddock or cod!" shouted the Duke, spitting out the words as though they made a bad taste in his mouth. "Cast your eyes, my dear Pelly, over there to the south."

The Pelican looked across the vast rolling estate and in the distance he saw a great river.

"That is the River Hamp!" cried the Duke. "The finest salmon river in the whole of Europe!"

"*Salmon!*" screeched the Pelican. "Not *salmon*? You don't really mean *salmon*?"

"It's *full* of salmon," the Duke said, "and I own it. You can help yourself."

Before he had finished speaking the Pelican was in the air. The Duke and I watched him as he flew full speed towards the river. We saw him circle over the water, then he dived and disappeared. A few moments later, he was in the air again, and he had a gigantic salmon in his beak.

I stood alone with the Duke on the lawn beside his great house. "Well, Billy," he said, "I'm glad they are all happy. But what about you, my lad? I am wondering if you happen to have just one extra special little wish all for yourself. If you do, I'd love you to tell me about it."

There was a sudden tingling in my toes. It felt as though something tremendous might be going to happen to me any moment.

"Yes," I murmured nervously. "I do have one extra special little wish."

"And what might that be?" said the Duke in a kindly voice.

"There is an old wooden house near where I live," I said. "It's called The Grubber and long ago it used to be a sweet-shop. I have wished and wished that one day somebody might come along and make it into a marvellous new sweet-shop all over again."

"Somebody?" cried the Duke. "What do you mean, *somebody*?" You and I will do that! We'll do it together! We'll make it into the most wonderful sweet-shop in the world! And *you*, my boy, will own it!"

Whenever the old Duke got excited, his enormous moustaches started to bristle and jump about. Right now they were jumping up and down so much it looked as though he had a squirrel on his face. "By Gad, sir!" he cried, waving his stick, "I shall buy the place today! Then we'll all get to work and have the whole thing ready in no time! You just wait and see what sort of a sweet-shop we are going to make out of this Grubber place of yours!"

It was amazing how quickly things began to happen
after that. There was no problem about buying the
house because it was owned by the Giraffe and the
Pelly and the Monkey, and they insisted upon giving it
to the Duke for nothing.

Then builders and carpenters moved in and rebuilt
the whole of the inside so that once again it had three
floors. On all these floors they put together rows and
rows of tall shelves, and there were ladders to climb up
to the highest shelves and baskets to carry what you
bought.

Then the sweets and chocs and toffees and fudges and nougats began pouring in to fill the shelves. They came by aeroplane from every country in the world, the most wild and wondrous things you could ever imagine.

There were Gumtwizzlers and Fizzwinkles from China, Frothblowers and Spitsizzlers from Africa, Tummyticklers and Gobwangles from the Fiji Islands and Liplickers and Plushnuggets from the Land of the Midnight Sun.

For two whole weeks the flood of boxes and sacks continued to arrive. I could no longer keep track of all the countries they came from, but you can bet your life that as I unpacked each new batch I sampled it carefully. I can remember especially the Giant Wangdoodles from Australia, every one with a huge ripe red strawberry hidden inside its crispy chocolate crust . . .

and the Electric Fizzcocklers
that made every hair on your
head stand straight up on
end as soon as you popped
one into your mouth . . . and
there were Nishnobblers and
Gumglotters and Blue
Bubblers and Sherbet Slur-
pers and Tongue Rakers,
and as well as all this, there
was a whole lot of splendid
stuff from the great Wonka
factory itself, for example
the famous Willy Wonka
Rainbow Drops – suck them
and you can spit in seven

different colours. And his
Stickjaw for talkative
parents. And his Mint
Jujubes that will give the boy
next door green teeth for a
month.

On the Grand Opening Day, I decided to allow all my customers to help themselves for free, and the place was so crowded with children you could hardly move. The television cameras and the newspaper reporters were all there, and the old Duke himself stood outside in the road with my friends the Giraffe and the Pelly and the Monkey watching the marvellous scene. I came out of the shop to join them for a few moments and I brought each of them a bag of extra special sweets as a present.

To the Duke, because the weather was a little chilly, I gave some Scarlet Scorchdroppers that had been sent to me from Iceland. The label said that they were guaranteed to make the person who sucked them as warm as toast even if he were standing stark naked at the North Pole in mid-winter. The moment the Duke popped one into his mouth, thick smoke came gushing out of the old boy's nostrils in such quantities that I thought his moustaches were going up in flames.

"Terrific!" he cried, hopping about. "Tremendous stuff! I'll take a case of them home with me!"

To the Giraffe I gave a bag of Glumptious Globgobblers. The Globgobbler is an especially delicious sweet that is made somewhere near Mecca, and the moment you bite into it, all the perfumed juices of Arabia go squirting down your gullet one after the other.

"It's wonderful!" cried the Giraffe as a cascade of lovely liquid flavours poured all the way down her long long throat. "It's even better than my favourite pink and purple flowers!"

To the Pelican I gave a big bag of Pishlets. Pishlets, as you probably know, are bought by children who are unable to whistle a tune as they walk along the street but long to do so. They had a splendid effect upon the Pelican, for after he had put one of them into his beak and chewed it for a while, he suddenly started singing like a nightingale. This made him wildly excited because Pelicans are not song-birds. No Pelican had ever been known to whistle a tune before.

To the Monkey I gave bag of Devil's Drenchers, those small fiery black sweets that one is not allowed to sell to children under four years old. When you have sucked a Devil's Drencher for a minute or so, you can set your breath alight and blow a huge column of fire twenty feet into the air. The Duke put a match to the Monkey's breath and shouted, "Blow, Monkey, blow!" A sheet of orange flame shot up as high as the roof of the Grubber house and it was wonderful.

"I've got to leave you now," I said. "I must go and look after my customers in the shop."

"We must go, too," said the Giraffe. "We have one hundred windows to clean before dark."

I said goodbye to the Duke, and then one by one I said goodbye to the three best friends I had ever had. Suddenly, we all became very quiet and melancholy, and the Monkey looked as though he was about to cry as he sang me a little song of farewell:

> *"We have tears in our eyes*
> *As we wave our goodbyes,*
> *We so loved being with you, we three.*
> *So do please now and then*
> *Come and see us again,*
> *The Giraffe and the Pelly and me.*
>
> *All you do is to look*
> *At a page in this book*
> *Because that's where we always will be.*
> *No book ever ends*
> *When it's full of your friends*
> *The Giraffe and the Pelly and me."*

The
Roald Dahl
Foundation

Throughout his life, Roald Dahl gave of his time and money to help people in need. When he died, his widow, Felicity Dahl established The Roald Dahl Foundation to continue this generous tradition. The Foundation's aim is to serve people in the UK in three major areas:

- **Literacy**, because it was Roald's crusade. Literacy is the most basic educational tool. It is also the passport to hours of pleasure. For many reasons, some people and some groups need extra help to help them to achieve this essential skill. The Foundation offers grants to a diverse group in this arena.

- **Neurology**, because brain damage has severely affected the Dahl family. Neurology funds specialise in the areas of epilepsy and head injury. In addition to our ongoing programme of individual grants to people in financial hardship, the Foundation grants funds to specially identified projects.

- **Haematology** because leukaemia was the cause of Roald's death. Our haematology grants target areas where funds are particularly hard to come by, but where the need is undeniably great. In addition to many individual grants, the Foundation supports large scale projects.

All monies donated to the Foundation are directed where they are required – to people in the UK with specific needs. If you would like to know more about us or help the Foundation in its work by making a donation then please write to us direct:

The Roald Dahl Foundation
92 High Street
Great Missenden
Buckinghamshire HP16 0AN
England

Registered Charity No. 1004230